OF FATE
AND FIRE

AMANDA
BOUCHET

To Nicole,
 I always love to see you! Thank you for reading and for being such a great supporter

A KINGMAKER CHRONICLES NOVELLA

of books! Lots of love ♡

Amanda B.

Copyright © 2021 by Amanda Bouchet

Cover art by Emily Wittig Designs

All rights reserved. Except as permitted under the U.S. Copyright Act of 1976, no part of this publication may be reproduced, distributed, or transmitted in any form or by any means, or stored in a database or retrieval system, without the prior written permission of the author.

This is a work of fiction. Names, characters, places, and incidents are either the products of the author's imagination or used fictitiously, and any resemblance to actual persons, living or dead, or business establishments, organizations, or locales is completely coincidental.

For Sébastien,

Thank you for brainstorming with me. You know how much you helped!

PROLOGUE

DECEMBER IN NORTHWESTERN CONNECTICUT—OR WHAT SOPHRONIA IRAKLIDIS AFFECTIONATELY CALLED "THE BOONIES"

Snow began falling as Sophie swept the crumbs from the last *Bûches de Noël* off the desks in her classroom. Decorating and eating a Yule log was her special treat for her French students as the semester wound down, and the kids who already knew her started talking about it from day one of the school year. They cared more about the sugar rush and being allowed to make a huge mess than about the Christmas dessert's origins, but if they could read her recipe in French and understand the directions and ingredients by the end of the lesson, she was happy.

Her mom and sister had come over to the saltbox house Sophie had plunged herself into debt for two years ago—in her defense, the little red colonial was irresistible—and helped her with the baking, filling, and rolling. She could make four cakes by herself in a weekend, maybe five, but ten was pushing it. Mom, Xanthe, and she had pulled up their sleeves and listened to old-timey Christmas music as they worked, sang along, and chatted. When Sophie started teaching, it became a holiday tradition for the three of them to "bake the boosh," as they called it, for Sophie's high-school French students, and she liked the idea of creating new traditions with her family just as much as she liked creating them in her classroom.

Of course, Mom and Xanthe tried to grill her about her love life. Since it was nonexistent, Sophie tossed the ball back at Xanthe, which her younger sister had appreciated about as much as stepping in dog poop with clean sneakers. Xanthe, at home for the weekend before college finals, might've had something juicy and exciting to share, but nope... As usual, her romance prospects were just as abysmal as Sophie's. For two women who couldn't deny being lucky in the looks department—they'd somehow inherited all the best parts of their striking, statuesque parents—they sure had trouble finding good boyfriends.

Sophie knew she was too tall, too blonde, too blue-eyed, too athletic, too traditional, too attached to her huge, overbearing family, too...everything. Xanthe was the same.

The sisters were convinced they intimidated the hell out of men, which seemed to have one result: the normal ones ran away from them, and the sleazy ones hit on them. As far as Sophie could tell, there was nothing in between, which left her home alone most nights either with a novel in her hands, binge watching something on TV, or grading homework. Usually, a lot of all three.

During the weekend cake-making fest, Mom started talking about "baking the boosh" with grandchildren soon, and Sophie nearly spit out the icing she'd been tasting. The men of Pinebury, Connecticut were going to have to seriously up their game before she got anywhere close to having children.

And she doubted her four brothers, all older than she, got the grandchildren comments from Mom, even though they were always popping in and out of Mom and Dad's house for something. Like dinner.

But her mother's half-joking comment had stuck with Sophie into her workweek, and for the first time since finishing her degrees and starting teaching, she almost wished settling down and having a family of her own didn't seem quite so far off or unrealistic.

Maybe it was her Greek roots—something genetically ingrained in her to crave a big, raucous, affectionate, opinionated family. Her grandparents on both sides had left a lot of their Greekness at the border when they immigrated to the United States, but the family had held on to tons of traditional recipes, a few bizarre superstitions, and unusual first names that had plagued both sisters since childhood. Her brothers got lucky. Alec, Seth, Jason, and

Hector. Well, maybe Hector wasn't so lucky. Poor Xanthe. She had the worst of it. No one ever knew to pronounce the *e* at the end, like in Persephone.

At school, everyone just called Sophie *Mademoiselle*, including most of the other faculty. Sophronia earned her strange looks, and Ms. Iraklidis rolled off the tongue about as easily as cold peanut butter.

Humming "Jingle Bell Rock"—which had been stuck in her head since the weekend—Sophie gave the desks a squirt with the cleaning spray she kept on hand and wiped them down before sweeping the floor of her classroom. Janitor Charlie already had enough work cleaning up after the students without her adding chocolaty fingerprints and powdered sugar to it.

When the kids decorated cakes, it was…an event. They'd had two Yule logs per class and free artistic license. Eating them was somehow even messier. But the *Bûches de Noël* had looked so pretty with the dark-chocolate shavings, red-and-green gumdrops, and little sugar-dusted marzipan pinecones. Sophie had taken pictures throughout the day and would add them to her *Album de l'année*, a scrapbook she made every year and kept in her classroom. She had six lined up now and planned on adding a career's-worth of them.

Finished at school, Sophie snagged her purse along with the two slices of cake she'd saved for her helper elves, Mom and Xanthe. She arrived home at the same time as a delivery person and signed for a package from her friend Aaron in California. He used to live in Michigan, but a big science technology company snapped him up right out of college—Aaron was a total genius—and he'd been there ever since, working for one of those *I'll-rule-the-world-someday-mwahahaha* types who scared the shit out of Sophie. They never cared about actual people.

Aaron wasn't like that, and she had no idea why he'd let himself get swept into an evil machine like Novalight Enterprises.

Sophie set everything on the hallway table and hung her bright-pink parka on the coatrack beside the door before making a quick detour to the kitchen to stick the cake in the fridge and put on the kettle. Curious as heck, she came straight back to the hallway and the package from Aaron, picking up the small, tightly taped-up box with her name on it.

She turned it over in her hands. Aaron and she had started out as pen pals through a middle school writing project and kept in touch over the years. He'd always liked hearing about her odd Greek stuff, like pretend spitting on people to ward off the evil eye and protect loved ones. Their contact had whittled down to holiday cards lately, and even that was pushing it. They definitely didn't send each other Christmas presents. Or Hanukkah presents—Aaron was Jewish. Or any presents at all. They'd never even met in person.

Sophie split the tape with a letter opener. She dug through some wadded-up yellow notepad paper and found another box, this one about the size of a matchbox, plain but pretty, and made from olive wood. She picked it up and opened it.

Her eyes widened. Inside, a glacial-blue crystal glowed.

Brightly. No, it *pulsed*. And it was *cold*. Its icy sting blasted over her like a winter wind. Goose bumps rose on her arms, and she shivered.

Confused and a little scared, Sophie set the wooden box on the table and backed away from it. The crystal seemed to shine from within. Was it poisonous? Radioactive? "What the heck, Aaron?" A weird vibration thrummed inside her, keeping her hair on end.

Grabbing the cardboard box the crystal arrived in, she looked through it for a card or note or something. Nothing.

No, wait. She frowned. Was that writing on the yellow notepad paper?

Sophie smoothed out one of the balls of paper and found half a word on it. Leaving the glowing crystal where it was, she took all the yellow papers into her living room and spread them out on the big Oriental rug her parents had given her as a housewarming present. The papers were a puzzle. Aaron had always liked puzzles. Sometimes, mostly during high school, he'd sent her letters in code, and it had taken her weeks to figure them out. This didn't look nearly as complicated, which meant he'd done it in a hurry.

In the end, heart racing and hands shaking, Sophie pieced together Aaron's message on the dozens of torn and crumpled pieces of paper. The scribbled writing only made sense to her in one order, and even then, she didn't understand much of anything.

Don't let Novalight get the Shard of Olympus. Too much power. Unstoppable. If it glows for you, you're Heracleidae. *I KNOW you are. The Greek gods are REAL. Contact Athena and GIVE THE SHARD BACK TO THE GODS OF OLYMPUS.*

Sophie swallowed hard, not wanting to believe a word she was seeing or how much danger Aaron must be in if he *stole* this precious, priceless, powerful object from his ambitious and frankly terrifying employer. How much danger *she* might be in.

Why would he do this to her? Because she had Greek origins? So did millions of people. Even Aaron, somewhere way back when on his mother's side. They'd thought it was cool they could both trace ancestors back to the Peloponnesus.

So then why...

She glanced toward the entryway for the millionth time in the past hour. The shard still glowed across the hallway from her, even brighter in the twilight of a December afternoon in New England. She felt the shard's cold, primordial power deep in her bones and knew that things weren't at all as they seemed. That maybe *she* wasn't.

Sophronia Iraklidis. Her first name meant sensible or wise. Her last name meant *son of Heracles*. Sure, she was a daughter, but whatever. The name was her father's. Most people knew the Roman version now—Hercules. The *Heracleidae* could be any of the ancient Greek hero's children and other descendants. And according to legend, he'd had plenty. Sophie's father had always insisted it was true, that they descended from *gods*, and she'd always thought he was full of it and kind of funny.

She wasn't laughing now.

In fact, she was terrified.

CHAPTER 1

Where am I? Why am I here?

Two questions Piers didn't like asking.

At least he still knew his name, although even that felt a little hazy at the moment.

Standing perfectly still, he looked from side to side, his eyes narrowing on the unfamiliar surroundings. *No*, not just unfamiliar. Totally and completely foreign.

Tension gripped him. His hands curled into fists. He couldn't process what he was seeing. He had no words for this.

All he knew was that he'd gone through a long dark

tunnel before popping out into a bright, blaring, incomprehensible metropolis.

This must be why babies entered the world wailing. If he weren't a grown man and a warrior, he'd want to wail, too. This place was awful.

Thank the gods, infants didn't remember. Life was traumatic enough already, especially when you had no idea what was happening. Or why. Something Piers could attest to right now—and then some.

Words magically flashed on the side of a tall building. The letters weren't familiar to him, but for some reason, he could still read and understand them instantly. *Welcome to the Big Apple.*

He frowned. That made about as much sense as the rest of this.

Sudden movement kicked up around him, in front and behind. He stayed where he was—apparently in the center of a wide, two-way thoroughfare. Strange, box-like units of transportation zoomed past without any horses or oxen to pull them. Many of them were yellow.

His heart galloping faster than a centaur, he turned in a slow circle. On all sides, buildings rose higher than any he'd ever seen in his full thirty-one Thalyrian year cycles. Endless windows climbed them, but instead of being deep-set, open arches, the windows contained reflecting glasses.

Suspicion stirred inside him. Windows like that were for people who hid things.

As he gazed skyward, an enormous, winged beast roared overhead, discharging a trail of smoke behind it.

Another shiny sky dragon crossed the first one's path, leaving writing above him. Piers stared at the two intersecting tracks of cloud fire. Did that *X* mean something?

Surrounded by objects and sights he'd never encountered let alone imagined, he knew with absolute certainty he was no longer in Thalyria—or at least, not on the known continent.

Was he dead? Could this be the Underworld?

That didn't make sense. The Underworld followed a pattern. You arrived on the Plain of Asphodel. If you had your obol—he checked his pocket, feeling the hard little nugget of the coin there—you handed it to Charon for passage across the River Styx. On the far side of the Styx, you either walked into a normal, everyday afterlife, or you followed the golden path to a glorious one in Elysium.

This definitely wasn't Elysium. And Piers didn't think it was the Underworld. Surely, he'd remember *dying*?

So, what was this Big Apple? And how did he end up here?

And *gods,* the noise. The place stank, too. Like everything else here, it was a smell he didn't recognize.

Jaw tight, eyes sharp, and hands ready for battle, Piers stayed where he was on the little island in the middle of the loud, zooming boxes. Buildings loomed over him like giants upon giants. More dragons soared overhead, their skywriting unrecognizable to him.

Worry thumped in his chest. If he knew what qualified as a threat here, his assessment of the situation would be far easier.

The last thing he remembered was traveling toward

Castle Tarva to try—*again*—to talk to his brother Griffin and Griffin's hot-headed harpy of a wife, Cat. They'd been holed up behind castle guards and high walls for days after successfully conquering a second realm and bringing Cat two thirds of the way to ruling all of Thalyria.

Fury stabbed Piers in the sternum. Cat's warmongering and lust for power had nearly gotten most of his family and friends killed. One friend didn't make it.

The knife in his chest twisted, and Piers growled, the sound covered by the terrible roar of the colossal city. Cat's fault. All of it.

Piecing his jumbled memories together made other things fall into place. Everything until... Was it mere minutes ago? Hours?

Uncertain, he shook his head. His youngest sister Kaia had been with him on the road to Tarva City. They'd seen Griffin and Cat in the distance, riding out to meet them. He'd been so angry. So worried and angry. His family in danger.

What else happened?

He pressed his lips together. He had no idea. Where had that hot, dusty day gone? Where had *he* gone, for that matter?

There was no dust in Apple. Only stone, glass, and metal. Barely a tree. And no sun beating down, either. He shivered. It wasn't *I'm-going-to-die-within-minutes-without-shelter* weather, but it sure as Hades wasn't hot. Everyone wore odd, puffy garments that covered them from hips to shoulders.

And earlier today... He'd had a plan in mind. Something important. What was it?

Hating his lack of clarity, Piers tensed as the horseless wagons stopped and other people joined him in the center of the thoroughfare. They didn't remain where he was, though. They kept walking toward the far side to where a small brightly lit striding man glowed pure white in a black box. More strange magic. He studied it, trying to understand the utility. The pedestrians gave him a wide berth as they passed, the kind you gave an unsavory ruffian or a drunkard covered in his own vomit and urine.

Scowling, Piers sniffed himself. Not fresh, but no vomit and urine. It could be worse.

At least the people of Apple looked more or less the same as Thalyrians, except strangely dressed and all seeming to be late for something. They raced by, heads down, many of them holding little rectangles that might've been glued to their fingers. No one carried any weapons that he could see, which made Piers itch to hide the sword strapped to his back and the knives in his belt. Were they why people avoided him?

He glanced down at himself. Belted tunic, boots, dust. His forearms were all scratched up for some reason. He worked his mouth from side to side, his jaw sore and aching. Most of him hurt in one way or another. He touched a hand to his throbbing nose. Blood came away on his fingers.

Wondering who he'd fought and why, Piers licked blood off his teeth and spat it in the street. A woman looked up from her rectangle and cringed away from him. She hurried to cross with the others.

Piers watched her go with a prickle of annoyance. He didn't attract females like his brothers seemed to, but he knew he wasn't repellant, either. Well, he might be a little repellant at the moment. He'd definitely been in a brawl, and most women didn't like that.

Wait. Maybe she could answer some questions for him, such as how far this Big Apple extended, and where he could find the person in charge of it.

He leaped after her just as a gigantic four-wheeled wagon charged forward. It swerved to avoid him, screeching. Piers reared back toward the middle where he'd been standing, but another metal cart blared a horrible noise, squealing to a stop just in front of him.

His pulse pounding, he scrambled back to the center island, wondering who'd come up with this aberration of a system. How did children survive here? He glanced at the small striding man. He was gone. A commanding red hand had overtaken the box he was in.

Ah. Got it.

White magic held the horseless wagons back so that people could hurry across this deathtrap. Red magic propelled the wagons forward.

The red sorcery swept the big yellow wagon that almost hit him away, but not before the man inside it made what Piers could only assume was a rude gesture out a half-open window, yelling at him in a language he somehow understood as if he'd been born to it. *Get out of the road, asshole!*

Piers stared after him. No one had spoken to him like that in enough time for him to forget how infuriating it was. Not only was he a prince now—because his family had godsdamned conquered a realm—but he led *armies*.

His brow furrowed. That didn't matter here, though. In Apple.

Information flashed everywhere, magically appearing and disappearing from building walls and huge freestanding panels. Some of it glowed, as though lit from within by different colored fires. The Magoi here must be very powerful, more favored by the gods than even the magic-wielders in Thalyria.

> BEEN IN AN ACCIDENT? CALL MO. MO'S YOUR MAN. HE'S GOT YOUR BACK, ESPECIALLY IF YOURS IS BROKEN.

> ALL YOU CAN EAT FRIED CHICKEN! EVERY FRIDAY NIGHT AT CLUCK CLUCK'S!

Reading and comprehending another language instantly would've been exciting if Piers had any idea what was happening. As it was, the strange ease just worried him.

Could this be Atlantis? Or Attica?

No, Attica lost its magic ages ago when the people there stopped worshipping the Olympians. Their lack of devotion caused their magic to dry up and the gods to abandon them. Only Athena supposedly still cared what went on in what she'd once considered *her* world.

Piers sent off a silent but heartfelt prayer to Athena, the

deity his family worshipped above all others. He wasn't too proud to ask for guidance, especially since he was incredibly lost right now.

He turned and scanned the magic signage behind him.

Broadway is back and better than ever! Go to heartbeatofnewyorkdiscounttickets.com for the best prices the internet has to offer!

New and Used Cars! Delany's Dealership has what you want at the prices you need! Special deals for veterans!

That last gigantic parchment on the wall had incredibly realistic drawings of the horseless wagons. *Cars.*

Piers grunted, internalizing the information. They had a name now. So did other things as he looked around. Reading the magic panels somehow helped him tame some of the unknown. Not enough, though. He still felt more lost than found.

A woman ran into the street while cars still moved forward, darting in and out of them like a cricket between hooves. One made a gods-awful noise. Someone yelled an insult, but she didn't even glance over her shoulder. Piers narrowed his eyes. Did she not know about the glowing-man, red-hand magic? She'd get herself killed.

She raced onto the central island and came to a screeching halt not far from him. The cars on the opposite side from where she'd started didn't provide an opening, whizzing by too fast for this cricket to risk launching herself into them. She sucked down air, her face red from cold and exertion. Piers swiftly took inventory. Tall. Blonde. A good runner—although he wasn't sure how in those little boots that hugged her ankles. Her puffy pink upper body apparel rose and fell on quick breaths as she frantically looked behind her.

Something in the woman's wide, frightened eyes made Piers's chest tighten. He followed her gaze, seeing two men step into the street, risking the oncoming cars to narrow the gap to the target they were obviously chasing.

"Shit." She spun in a half circle, feverishly looking for a way off the central island that didn't involve certain death —or at the very least, broken bones. Grimacing, she gathered herself to run.

Piers's protective instincts roared to life, and he reached for the woman just as she decided to throw all caution to the wind. His hand closed around her upper arm, stopping her from rushing headlong into traffic. She whirled on him with a gasp.

Bright blue eyes shot even wider than before. So blue. They punched into him like twin lightning bolts and stole the breath from his lungs.

"Don't cross yet." He sounded just like the people all around him. Since that went far beyond luck, he knew it was sorcery. "You have to wait for the striding man to hold back the metal wagons."

She gaped at him. "What? Let go of me!" She started twisting.

Piers turned his grip to stone, even though he didn't want to hurt her. "You'll get yourself killed."

"*They'll* kill me!" She glanced sideways at the oncoming men.

"Why?"

"*Why?*" Her jaw dropped farther. "Because they're hired thugs, and someone paid them to!"

Piers nodded. That was good enough for him to defend her. She could be lying, but he didn't think so. Something about her bright, inflated attire and tight little head covering with the multicolored zigzags running across it told him she was trustworthy, while the burly men in dark clothing hunting down a lone woman probably weren't the good guys.

"Stay here. Stay behind me," Piers said.

Her delicate brows snapped together. "Why?" She glanced toward the two big warriors. "I have to get out of here."

Piers followed her frightened gaze again. He had to admit, the two men looked formidable. Large. Muscular. One was blond. The other had brown hair. Beyond that, they looked interchangeable. Same size, shape, and posture. He wouldn't have minded having his brothers with him right now, but since he was alone, he'd handle it.

"Stay," he repeated, letting her arm go with a little squeeze to help convince her.

She wrenched away from him. "I'm not a dog!" Her frosty indignation hit him at the same time as the cold wind barreling down the thoroughfare. She looked him up and down, probably seeing his goose bumps. "Just because you escaped from…I don't know…the set of *Gladiator* doesn't mean you get to order me around like some Roman general!"

While her words themselves made sense to him, Piers had no idea what she meant by any of that except for *general*—which was true. But right now, he didn't have time to deal with his questions. The warriors arrived on the central island, barely sparing him a glance as they focused on the woman.

"Nowhere left to run," the fair-haired one said with a satisfied chuckle.

Her breath shuddered. She backed toward the cars racing behind her, her golden hair flying on the wind, her eyes wide with terror.

"Stay!" Piers growled.

Her eyes snapped to his. She swallowed and stopped moving.

"Hand it over." The second man's flinty stare was as dark as his hair and clothing. "Give up the crystal, and you can stop running. Don't you want to go home to your family for Christmas? Or maybe we should pay *them* a little visit?"

Behind Piers, she sucked in a sharp breath. Anger sparked inside him, and he placed himself even more squarely in front of her.

"I think you should leave now," Piers ground out. The hired ruffians could go back the same way they'd come, cars and all. The magic would change soon anyway. It alternated.

The blond jerked his chin at Piers. "This isn't your problem, Zorba. Go back to the Theater District."

The other man moved closer, holding out his hand and beckoning for this crystal the woman must have in her possession. "There's no reason for the same thing to happen to you as to your friend in California. He took something that wasn't his and sent it to you. He should never have put you in the middle of this. All my employer wants is the crystal. He doesn't give a shit about a French teacher from Connecticut. And you"—his eyes flicked to Piers—"get out of the way, asshole."

This insult was obviously in fashion. Piers was going to have to start using it. "No. Leave her alone and back away unless you want to lose that hand...asshole."

Piers didn't check over his shoulder for confirmation. If the woman wanted to hand over the crystal, she would. Instead, she'd led two ruffians on a difficult chase they were obviously sick of. Good for her. He smiled.

Both men's demeanors shifted. Half a step back, shoulders stiffer, necks shorter, brows lowered. Had they only just now noticed the broken nose and blood on his teeth? People weren't very observant in Apple.

Traffic stopped, and the woman bolted. *Zeus's bollocks!* Piers grabbed the blond who leaped after her, hauling him back with a snarl. The dark-haired one darted wide, jumped a barrier, and chased her.

The ruffian he'd caught had some combat training. It was enough to break free and land a blow to Piers's ribs. The son of a Cyclops must've thought that was it, because he tried to sprint away again. Piers yanked him back and punched him in the jaw. The man stood there like an idiot, his mouth ajar. Since he was pressed for time, Piers shifted his weight and cracked his elbow into the man's nose. Not the most sporting of moves, but effective. The big thug squealed like a piglet. He clearly didn't know how to fight someone who could fight him back, which was probably why he was preying on a weaponless and fleeing woman.

Pink's frightened stare and panicked little breaths struck him anew, right in the gut this time. Piers spun into a kick, slamming the man in the head with zero remorse and probably harder than he needed to. The lout crumpled.

"Asshole." Piers turned without a backward glance and ran after the dark-haired man and the woman.

He barely beat the magic and made it across the road before the glowing red hand propelled the traffic forward. He pumped his arms, pushing for as much speed as he dared with frost slicking parts of the hard ground. Cold air filled his lungs, biting his chest from the inside out. He grimaced. What a time to have an aching everything.

Just when he feared he'd lost her, Piers caught a flash of bright color. He followed, slipping once and nearly falling. People jumped out of his way. That was helpful, but not knowing the lay of the land infuriated him. In the blink of an eye, the blue-eyed beauty could disappear, and he'd have no idea where to go, or how to find her.

Or if she was still in danger.

Pink skidded around a sharp corner. Piers followed, sliding but somehow keeping his balance and coming out running. The woman moved fast, with nimble surefootedness even on the sometimes-icy surfaces. Piers barely gained on her. He didn't see the second warrior. *Warrior* might not be the term merited, but he wasn't about to underestimate the second ruffian-for-hire just because the first had been incompetent.

Pink ran as though Zeus's thunderbolts dogged her heels, and Piers chased her down another narrow street between high buildings. The times he lost sight of that bright, puffy garment and bouncing yellow mane made his pulse race even faster. She turned a corner up ahead, and he pushed himself to his limit, his lungs working like bellows. He turned the same corner just in time to see the dark-haired man pounce out at her from a side alley. The thug slammed into her, sending her sprawling across the pavement.

Piers didn't know where the word *pavement* came from and didn't care. His heart exploded with her scream. He drove into the man like a battering ram, shoulder first, head lowered. They scraped across the pavement. *Holy gods!* He exhaled sharply.

Piers blocked out the pain of several fresh, raw abrasions and jumped to his feet. So did the ruffian. The man drew a knife. Piers drew his sword.

The other man's eyes narrowed. "That's not real."

"Try it," Piers growled.

The coward tossed his knife aside and pulled out a smallish black thing Piers could only assume was a better weapon. But what kind? He didn't see a blade. Was this magic?

"Get down!" Pink screamed.

Piers ducked as she darted in and slammed a wooden plank into the thug's hand. The man dropped the weapon.

Piers kicked it aside. The black thing slid under a big

refuse receptacle that smelled even worse than the rest of Apple. The hired thug leaped for his discarded knife. Faster by two steps, Piers swept it up first, finding himself in the pleasant position of being double-bladed while his enemy had nothing.

"Who the hell *are* you?" The man's eyes darted to the alley he'd just popped out of. If he thought Piers was going to let him run back down it, he had another guess coming. "Fucking lunatic."

"I like that name better than Zorba," Piers said.

Pink laughed. The sudden burst sounded a bit hysterical, but she still laughed, and Piers's chest swelled with it.

He glanced at her. "Does he live or die?" Piers figured he should give her the choice, since he didn't know much about this. He kept his blades pointed in the right direction.

Her frantic laughter abruptly wilted. "Wait? You're serious?"

Piers didn't kill for sport or enjoy it, but when it came down to eliminating threats that could come back to haunt him—or her—he was dead serious. He nodded.

"You can't just *kill* people," she whisper-hissed, moving closer to him. She gripped his arm, trying to move him away from the ruffian. *Warrior* was definitely a stretch, and Piers wouldn't credit the man with the moniker. Either of his younger sisters could've kicked this man's arse from here to Olympus. As for his brothers... Griffin would've snapped his neck, no questions asked. Carver would've gutted him.

Something deep inside Piers shifted uncomfortably at

the idea of Griffin. But why? He'd been riding toward Griffin and Cat, and then… Nothing. He didn't remember what happened.

Pink tugged again, but Piers didn't budge. "Come on," she said, pulling harder.

"He was going to kill you." Piers wasn't the bloodthirsty sort, but he was tempted to make an exception if it meant keeping the woman safe. "He'll try again."

"No! I wasn't! I won't!" The man shook his head, raising his hands in surrender. "I just want the crystal. That's it. Then it's over."

"Can you give him the crystal?" Piers asked.

She shook her head, her blue eyes wide again.

"Then he has to die." The ruffian-for-hire had threatened her. Her family. What if she had a large family like he did? He would do anything to protect them.

Pink gaped at him. She did that a lot. "I don't know what circus decided to spit you out, or what wardrobe from Narnia, but life has *value* here. And murder has consequences. *You can't just kill people*," she insisted.

"Fine." Annoyed, Piers flipped his sword around and brought the hilt down on the man's temple. Thug Two slumped to the side, unconscious near the refuse pile along with the rest of the garbage. With any luck, he'd have forgotten this coveted crystal when he woke up as well as the blonde woman. He might also have forgotten his own name, but Piers didn't consider that his problem.

CHAPTER 2

Sophie's life had gone from normal, if a little boring, to utterly insane. How could a handful of days make such a difference? She kept wondering if she'd blinked and woken up in an alternate reality—one where she had to flee her house in the middle of the night when she heard people breaking into it, where hopping from hotel room to hotel room in the city under false names didn't throw off the people chasing her, where she ran for her life—*repeatedly*, where incredibly hot—if really strange—men jumped in to help her for no apparent reason, where Greek gods were real, where...

She started breathing so fast her vision turned spotty.

Where she was about to have a breakdown.

"Breathe. Slowly." The man put his hand between her shoulder blades. He didn't press, or rub, or do anything, really, but the heat from his hand gave her something to concentrate on other than the ice-cold panic beating through her system.

Or maybe that was the freezing-cold crystal in her pocket. The Shard of Olympus. The darn thing wasn't a rock. It was an icicle. And it *never* melted.

Sophie drew her shoulders back and took a deep breath. She shook herself out a little. The man let his hand fall away from her, and oddly, she missed it. But her pulse was getting back to normal, and they had to get the hell out of here. Novalight's lackey could wake up any second. Or more could come. He seemed to have an endless supply of minions.

"We need to go." She glanced from side to side at the miraculously still people-free alley, at a loss for what to do next after days of exhausting herself and her resources. She was a French teacher, not a millionaire expert at subterfuge.

Nerves made that odd, low buzzing hum in her veins again. It was almost electric. Her fingers tingled with it, heating. She shoved her hands in her pockets.

"Do you, um, have a place in the city?" Her latest hotel room had been compromised—hence today's run-for-your-life episode. She'd lost a toothbrush and her pajamas, but everything else was in her car, which she'd parked in a whole different neighborhood.

The man shook his head.

Darn. Maybe he was from New Jersey.

At least these two hired guns from Novalight Enterprises would think twice about chasing her down again. She'd given everyone who'd come after her the slip so far, but she'd never left anyone unconscious. She giggled.

"Are you well?" Her rescuer's gray eyes filled with concern for her. A cowlick lifted his black hair away from his forehead, even though parts of it were long enough to brush his cheekbones. He had a strong brow. A strong jaw. A strong—and swollen—nose. A strong everything, really. *Wow*, those arms were like tree trunks. And he didn't even look cold when he was wearing...a toga?

Sophie swallowed more inappropriate laughter. "No. I don't think I'm well. Are you?" He looked as if he'd been hit by a bus on the way to a costume party.

"I'm...not entirely certain," he answered.

Well, that made two of them.

He offered his arm as though they were headed to the dance floor for a waltz. Sophie automatically slipped her hand through the crook at his elbow, and they strolled out of the alley to the music of a police siren in the distance. Hopefully, the cops were after someone else.

When they'd put a block between themselves and the Novalight security agent, Sophie steered them east toward where she'd left her car the night before. She didn't know New York that well and had figured her car was safest in a central neighborhood. Trying to remain positive, she told herself it was still there.

"Do you have a name?" she asked the man beside her.

She was glad he'd stuck around so far and kind of dreaded the moment he'd leave her.

He shrugged.

"Does that mean no?"

"Everyone has a name," he answered.

"Well, can I have yours?" Sophie let a teasing note creep into her voice. This guy was taking being an enigma to a whole new level.

He pursed his lips. Full lips. Extremely kissable. A little tinged with blue now that he was cooling down from the fight. Poor guy. He wasn't dressed for December.

Sophie couldn't believe she was noticing her companion's physical attributes when her life was in danger and stopping Novalight from taking over the world was apparently at stake, but it was too hard not to. Her rescuer was glaringly handsome, even all scratched and bruised, with a somewhat freshly broken nose, and in his bizarre Caesar outfit. All that was missing was the laurel wreath crown.

Her brows flew up. She stopped and pulled him to a halt. "Do you not remember? Do you have amnesia or something?" Judging by the state of him, she was pretty sure he'd been knocked in the head a few times.

He tugged, moving them along. "Or something."

Sophie took a quick step to keep up with his long-legged stride. "I'll give you a name, then. A temporary one —just till you remember your own."

"Why?" he asked.

Why? "So I can stop calling you *The Man* in my head. Or Caesar."

"Caesar's not bad." He'd never heard it before, but he liked it.

She grimaced. "Please, no. Even dressed like that."

He glanced down at himself. "The people of Apple don't like strong names?"

Sophie did her best fish-out-of-water impression. When her throat stung from the cold, dry air, she snapped her mouth shut. This was getting weirder by the second, and her current life was already weird enough. "Okay. I'll call you Bob."

"*Bob?*" He couldn't have looked more incredulous if she'd suggested Yoda or Spock.

"Bob's a good name," she defended. She had an uncle on her mom's side who'd escaped the Greekness and ended up with Robert for a first name. Bob for short. Half her family couldn't pronounce it and called him Boob instead.

"Bob sounds like something you'd name a goat."

"Okaaaay. How 'bout Bill?" she suggested.

"Now I'm to be called the mouth of a duck?" His jaw visibly tightened. "Fine. I have a name. You might've heard of me, in which case, maybe you can point me in the direction of home." He took a deep breath. "Piers. Piers of Sinta. Gamma of the realm and third in line for the throne."

Sophie mashed her lips together, quelling a chuckle. Was he a performer? She appreciated a person so devoted to their craft that they stayed in character despite near-freezing weather and a very-real fight with a power-drunk megalomaniac's henchmen, but it was time to drop the act. "Yeah, I don't think I can point you in the direction of

The Realm. Sorry. Got any other information, Piers of Sinta?"

His eyes narrowed. "Are you mocking me?" It didn't look like anyone mocked him often, or easily.

"Maybe." She squeezed his arm to ease the sting. "Sorry. I come from a big family. Teasing is second nature."

Something in his eyes both brightened and darkened. It was pure devotion. Gut-twisting worry. Sophie bit her lip, shocked by how hard her heart flipped over at the pained expression flickering across his face. "So, I guess you don't have amnesia?"

His reply was a low grunt. How helpful.

A moment later, he asked, "Do *you* have a name?"

"Why?" she teased. She couldn't help it.

His—*Piers's*—lips twitched. "So I can stop calling you Pink in my head. Or *The Woman*."

Sophie laughed. Considering how scared she'd just been, this whole conversation seemed surreal to her—as surreal as being helped by a gladiator named Piers of Sinta.

"It's Sophie. Sophronia Iraklidis."

"Now *that's* a normal name," he said with a firm nod of his head.

Oddly, he was dead serious. "You're the only one who thinks so."

"The prudent and wise descendant of Heracles." He cocked his head, his coal-dark hair catching the first snowflakes as they fell. "If you're Magoi, why not defend yourself?"

Magoi? Sophie was so confused right now, it wasn't even funny. She was also getting really cold after the adrenaline rush and flat-out sprinting. She shivered. "Are you a classics professor? Were you at a reenactment or something?"

His nose wrinkled. "Or something."

They continued toward Midtown. Piers obviously liked his secrets. She decided not to push. She had a thumb-sized secret of her own icing a hole in her pocket right now. Her teeth started chattering, the cold attacking her from inside and out.

"We should get you to shelter." He made a beeline for the nearest shop. It was a frilly underwear boutique. Sophie nudged him one door farther down the avenue. As luck would have it, it was a men's clothing store.

"Do you have anything to change into?" she asked. Somehow, she knew he didn't. If it weren't complete insanity, she'd think this was a bit of a Thor situation, but instead of finding a mouthwatering Norse god with a magic hammer, she'd found a tall, dark, fine-as-hell swordsman who seemed to have gotten lost on his way to the Trojan War. The whole thing was starting to feel less strange by the second—which was strange in itself. Sophie supposed people were adaptable. Human beings could get used to anything, good or bad.

Letting go of Piers's arm, she headed through the automatic revolving door. Piers stayed on the other side, eyeing the transparent glass with suspicion. His hand slid toward his sword.

Sophie did the full circle and went back for him, the damp cold outside hitting her like a snowball to the face. She reached for his arm, drew him into the little moving wedge, and they shuffled sideways together, nearly chest to chest, until she stepped out and pulled him into the blissfully warm shop. The heater was going full blast, especially near the entrance.

Piers held out his hand and moved his fingers, as though trying to catch the heat circulating around them. He glanced back at the doorway, his eyes narrowing. If the revolving door were a dragon, he would draw his sword and slay it. Forthwith. She grinned at him.

He frowned. "Are you from the Ice Plains? Is that where we are?"

It was certainly cold enough to ice things over, but Sophie shook her head. "I'm from Connecticut."

"Cunnetakit." His frown deepened. "This place is new to me."

"I'll bet." Her lips twitched. She didn't want Piers to think she was mocking him, but it was hard not to get a kick out of his mistrust of a revolving door and obvious fascination with central heating. "Do you have any other clothes?" she asked again.

He shook his head. "I wouldn't mind one of these puffy things everyone is wearing." He glanced at her pink parka. Hesitantly, he reached out and poked the zipper with a really tanned finger for New York in December. "Do you have another one of these?"

"Uh…not on me. But I'm pretty sure we can find something here."

"Do they accept coins?" he asked, glancing around the store.

She rolled her lips in to keep from smiling. "Well, you'd definitely need a lot of them."

His color rose. "I'm a little lost here…Sophronia. I might not have the means to pay." Piers started for the exit.

"Hold on." Sophie grabbed his arm and steered him toward the jackets. "You just saved my life. Literally. I have money in the bank, and the least I can do is buy you some proper winter clothing."

"You don't need to buy me anything." He looked as if she'd tried to call him Bob again.

"I know I don't *need* to, but I want to. Don't people repay debts in Sinta?" Wherever the hell that was.

A muscle ticked near his eye. "They don't pay a prince back for helping a lady in distress."

"Oh, you're a prince now?" Sophie laughed. "That's right—third in line for the throne."

He glared.

"Sorry." She cleared her throat. "I'm sure you can pay me back from the…eh…royal coffers. But let's just get what you need for now."

He finally agreed, but it was like pulling teeth from a rhinoceros. Sophie had never met a more stubborn man in her life.

Or one more sinfully handsome. They finished with Piers in a cream-colored V-neck sweater that hugged his strong torso (she could see his six pack—possibly eight—practically waving at her from under the material), dark cargo pants (he really liked all the pockets), solid leather boots (he did *not* enjoy laces instead of buckles), and a navy-blue winter jacket they'd had to get in XL because nothing else fit Piers's tall, muscular frame. Those arms and shoulders… Sophie had snuck so many looks her eyeballs were tired from all the bouncing back and forth.

She had to admit, Piers looked pretty darn amazing in the clothes they'd picked out for him, even though he definitely needed a shower. And probably a doctor. At the very least, some disinfectant. She'd dig a painkiller out of her purse when she could stop staring, although he'd probably refuse her "sorcery" and just look around for the next enemy to wallop.

Sophie hid her smile, especially because Piers didn't seem all that comfortable in his new outfit. He kept plucking at his sweater and muttering about how formfitting it was. She wasn't the only one gawking. The salesman was just as impressed with Piers's physique as she was. The salesman wanted to *be* him, even with all the cuts and bruises. It was cute and funny. They got ten percent off, which was even better.

When they'd finished, Sophie paid, although Piers didn't look at ease with that, and he really didn't understand the idea of a credit card. She wasn't sure she should be using her card with an evil genius like Novalight tracking her for the shard, but what choice did she have? It wasn't as if she had oodles of cash stuffed down her bra. Besides, New York was huge. She'd stop at the nearest ATM to get money for a new hotel room and food, not use her card again for a while, and leave the neighborhood. Rinse and repeat, as necessary—or until her funds ran out. At least now, she had a bodyguard.

With Piers just outside in the now heavily falling snow

—and discovering what *waterproof* meant for his new boots and jacket—Sophie pretended to have left something at the register and zipped back into the shop for another full change of clothing and some men's underwear in what she hoped was the right size. Piers had saved her *life*. He could at least get two outfits and some boxers out of it. While she did that, he went through the revolving door three times.

"Mastered the door now, have you?" she asked with a smile as she joined him on the icy sidewalk.

Piers gave the storefront a last long look. "There are some very interesting things here in Apple. The Magoi must be extremely powerful, and you don't even see them. I'm impressed."

She wasn't sure about the whole Magoi thing, but… "Apple? As in, the Big Apple?"

Nodding, he asked, "Is Apple just one city or the whole continent?"

Eh… "Actually, it's New York City. The Big Apple is just a nickname. And it's only a tiny part of the continent."

He stopped, his brow knitting. "This continent must be huge."

"North America?" She shrugged and tugged him along. Her car wasn't far now. "It's pretty big. And there are six more continents around the world."

"Seven whole continents?" He shook his head in apparent wonder. "And nothing is god touched?"

"God touched? What does that mean?"

"Beyond the known continent—where you can't go. No one goes there."

"Why not?"

Piers looked at her as though *she* were the crazy one saying crazy things every two seconds. "Because you don't come back."

She frowned in confusion. "Like…the Bermuda Triangle?"

"Like *everywhere* beyond the established borders."

It was Sophie's turn to stop and stare. Was he saying he came from a finite place hemmed in on all sides by some sort of deity or power? It sounded more like Asgard by the second—or at least how she imagined it after watching *Thor* for the she-wasn't-sure-how-manyth time. A woman had to entertain herself on weekend nights at home.

She took a steadying breath, trying to understand what Piers was saying. Acceptance had been growing all morning, but now, she started truly believing he really wasn't from here. Here, as in, Earth. He looked human enough, but what if the hot guy she'd apparently picked up between bouts of running for her life was an alien? What if this gorgeous façade was some kind of glamour, and he was actually slimy and covered in scales?

No. She refused to believe that. Or she didn't want to, which was different, but at this point, she didn't care. Besides, if Piers was an alien, he probably needed her help right now just as much as she needed his. "Okay. So, if you're not from Earth, where *are* you from? Where's this Sinta?"

"Thalyria," he answered.

Zero hesitation. Zero thought. Not that Sophie was an

expert lie detector, but he seemed like he was telling the truth.

"I've never heard of it." She doubted anyone had.

He shrugged. "I'd never heard of Apple, either. Or...New York City." The words sounded foreign on his tongue.

Sophie slowly nodded, trying to hide the tremor in her hands as she readjusted her reality. Wasn't her reality already off-kilter enough these days?

But Piers wasn't making this up. She knew it somehow, just as she knew the ice shard's cold, hard power pulsing too close to her skin for comfort was no joke. None of this was.

"Yeah, you're definitely not from Earth. *Everyone* knows New York. It's just...one of those facts of life." She started walking again, deciding to embrace the weirdness rather than try to fight it. She needed to conserve her energy for the next time Novalight's goons came knocking, because she had no doubt they would. At least she and Piers fit in better now that his Caesar outfit was out of sight.

She almost missed the belted robe. Piers pulled that look off like a champ. He'd kept his sword, stuffing it and the whole harness contraption under his jacket. The hilt poked up over his shoulder now. That was still a bit conspicuous, but hey, this was New York. Tons of weird stuff happened here.

The knot in Sophie's stomach unraveled for the first time in days. Peace settled over her. Maybe it was wrong of her—she always figured she'd be more the *I-am-woman-hear-me-roar* type—but she was just happy not to be alone anymore. Piers seemed willing to help and didn't appear to have anything else to do. She'd called in sick for the last week of school and run away from Pinebury to try to keep her family out of danger, but Sophie wasn't used to being on her own, and she didn't like it. Sure, she lived by herself, but that wasn't the same as being *alone*. Especially at Christmas. It was almost as if Piers had been sent by the Powers That Be just when she needed him most.

The Greek gods are REAL.

Sophie shivered, a chill racing down her neck and spine. Suddenly, Aaron didn't seem so crazy with his whole *you're-Heracleidae, contact-Athena* message, and Piers might be the only thing that made sense. She had the glowing, ice-cold, apparently *magical* Shard of Olympus in her pocket. And by her side, she had a man who looked and acted as if he'd just popped straight out of antiquity, protecting her. What were the chances of that?

Don't let Novalight get the Shard of Olympus. Too much power. Unstoppable.

Worry shuddered through her again. In Greek mythology, the gods were always watching, manipulating, and interfering. They were violent, remorseless, jealous, horrible, and hella-messed-up for the most part, but sometimes, they did surprisingly good things. Like Prometheus. He defied the gods, stealing fire from Mount Olympus and giving it to humans so that they could cook and keep warm with it. Sure, that brought down Pandora and her Box on humanity and got poor Prometheus chained to a rock in Tartarus, but his intentions were good.

Supposedly, Sophie's ancestor Heracles freed Prometheus from his punishment, but she had a hard time believing it—and everything else. She thought the Titan was still there—if *he* and *there* even existed—chained up and getting his immortal liver pecked out by a giant eagle every day.

And if Prometheus could take that, then she could take this.

Sophie pulled her shoulders back, finding courage from the myth her father used to tell her at bedtime. She'd take her current weirdness over Prometheus's fate any day, along with a bowl of soup, a hotel room that didn't have cockroaches, and a plan. Assuming she didn't need to check herself into a psychiatric unit, she had to figure out how to contact Athena, and she was pretty sure the internet didn't have a workable answer to: *How do you call a Greek god*.

CHAPTER 3

More sorcery. This time, it was called a shower.

Piers stood under the hot stream of water, groaning. Sophronia probably thought he was dying in here, but he couldn't help himself. It was incredible. The whole room was. Human waste flushed away at the press of a button. Water turned on and off with a flick of the wrist. Bright lights that required neither oil nor wick. Soap that smelled just like something you could eat. He wanted to lick it off his arm and see what it tasted like. He didn't, but he was tempted. The bubbles were hard to resist.

The only thing intruding on Piers's bathroom bliss was

wishing he could tell his family about the wonders of this place. His sisters, especially, would love it. Egeria would explore every nook and cranny, discovering how things worked. Jocasta would quietly observe until she produced a pearl of insight that would transform everyone's vision of things. And Kaia. His heart pinched. Her boundless excitement would be contagious.

Piers squeezed his eyes shut. Would he ever see his family again? Not only his three sisters, but Griffin and Carver, too? His parents? He'd always lived in the middle of a constant throng of people, activity, and projects, and suddenly finding himself lost and alone—well, not quite alone—made it hard to breathe sometimes. The truth was, he didn't know how to get back to them—if he even *could* get back to them. And it was hard to make a plan when he didn't know where he was or why he'd ended up here.

The one thing he did know was that humans didn't travel between the gods' worlds. Gods could. Magical creatures could. But not regular people. Which meant something had gone colossally wrong.

Knowing where he was would help. "Earth" meant nothing to him, but maybe what Sophronia called her home world was just a different name for something he *did* know. It was too big for Atlantis, too pleasant—despite the ruffians chasing an innocent woman—for Tartarus, and he'd already ruled out the Underworld. It definitely wasn't Thalyria, even if he took into consideration the places he wasn't familiar with, such as the nearly inaccessible Ice Plains. The northern reaches of Thalyria weren't quite god touched, but they were almost dangerous enough to be so, especially with Mount Olympus looming in the distance.

Which brought him back to Attica. Athena's favored world.

But that didn't add up, either. There was magic here. Wasn't there? Sophronia called it technology, but to him, it seemed synonymous so far.

"Are you okay in there?" she called through the door.

Piers reluctantly turned off the water. "Your turn in just a moment," he called back.

He'd been hesitant to go up into this hired chamber with her, but she'd insisted, and in the end, he didn't appear to have the correct currency to pay for his own space. He'd pulled out several gold coins, but Sophronia had just closed his hand back around them, her eyes wide, telling him they'd look into that later, when they had time.

"There's no hurry. I took a shower this morning." She paused, laughing a little. The sound made Piers's skin tighten. "Although, that was *before* I got tackled in a filthy New York alley."

It was suddenly hard not to picture her in this very shower. Warm water, soap and suds, hands gliding all over her wet, heated body. A low groan escaped him as he pushed at the sliding doors, opening them and stepping out of the box, the perfectly transparent glass now clouded with steam and moisture.

"Are you sure you're all right? You're pretty beat up. That nose..."

Cool air swirled over him, and Piers reached for the fluffy white drying cloth the hotel provided. His nose ached somewhat. The rest of him seemed fine. He didn't *look* exactly fine—the miraculously clear mirror in the bathroom told him so—but he'd been more broken and battered than this. War wasn't fun, which was why he'd wanted to avoid more of it.

He cinched the big cloth around his waist, frustrated. What wasn't he remembering?

Meet Griffin and Cat.

Avoid more bloodshed.

Protect his family.

Griffin and his ferocious wife had already conquered two realms. Did they really need a third? Cat's ambition would get his family killed. He needed to stop it—stop *her*—before it was too late.

He could've sworn he'd found a solution. What was it? And how had it landed him here?

He looked around the steam-clouded bathroom, but no clues jumped out at him. Since there were extra drying cloths, he used a second one to scrub his hair. "*That nose* is fine," he finally answered. "I fixed it."

"What? Like, yourself?"

He scoffed. "I hardly need a healer for that."

"Okaaaay." Pause. "Do you like the other outfit?"

Piers winced. Sophronia had purchased more clothing for him when he hadn't been looking. He blamed the wonder of waterproof and that fascinating zipper contraption. It wasn't that he was ungrateful. Sophronia was kind and thoughtful. He just didn't want her spending her money on him, and especially on useless items, such as those thin, tiny pants. What was a man supposed to do with those things?

"Everything's perfect," he called back. "Thank you."

He donned the same cargo pants and sweater he'd worn before. They were still fresh enough. Finished in the bathroom, he hung up the drying cloths, finger combed his hair, and pulled open the door. Sophronia was right on the other side of it.

He stopped short, warmth surging through him.

She sucked in a breath. "Sorry." She backed up a step. "It was just... We were talking."

Desire stirred, a thudding pulse low in his abdomen. Piers hadn't stood this close to a woman who aroused him in what felt like years. Maybe it *was* years. He spent all his time between the knowledge temples and the battlefield. Women seemed to like a warrior better than a scholar, at least in his world, but he'd always leaned more toward scrolls than swords. And if he wasn't battling, he wasn't sure he looked up from ink and parchment often enough to even notice who might be around.

"Please." He sounded as if he'd swallowed a handful of rocks. "This is your room. Stand where you like."

"It's *our* room," she corrected. "At least, until we figure things out."

Piers nodded, tension sizzling inside him. There was only one bed, but he'd sleep on the floor. Or maybe he just wouldn't sleep. He'd keep watch. He'd watch her.

Well, he'd try not to stare, but he was pretty sure he'd fail.

"Shower time," Sophronia said brightly, gathering a little pink bag from the bedside table. "I'm going to wash that trash-filled alley out of my hair while you settle in, and then we'll... I don't know." She shrugged. "Make a plan? Too bad *Run-For-Your-Life 101* wasn't a class in college. In retrospect, it would've been way more useful than French literature."

Piers stared at her, fascinated and confused. "You say the strangest things. I don't know what they mean half the time."

"Oh. Well, men like a mysterious woman." She grinned and shut the door to the bathroom, leaving him on the other side, alone, and thinking only one thing: *he* liked Sophronia Iraklidis. Probably more than he should.

They sat in what Sophronia told him was a *café*, drinking something called *coffee*, and eating something called *croissants*. It was good but not very filling. Piers wanted lamb, hearty vegetables, and thick brown bread. But since he was dependent on her little pieces of green paper to pay for their fare, he kept his mouth shut. He'd eat mutton the next time he came across it. Until then, he'd starve.

Snow still fell outside. He'd only seen snow once in his life before, on a scouting trip to the very north of Sinta during the rainy season. It had gotten cold enough for the rain to turn to snow. It hadn't stuck to the ground, as it did here, coating everything in a dull white blanket that seemed to suck all the sounds from the world. Inside the eating establishment, it was noisy in comparison, which made their low conversation seem even more intimate. He liked being ensconced in a private *tête-à-tête* with Sophronia. She'd said a few words in French to the waiter and filled Piers's mind with another complete language. If that wasn't magic, he didn't know what was.

Still, Sophronia denied being Magoi. Or knowing anything about magic.

"You can eat it, you know." She pushed her plate toward him. "Half was enough for me. I'm too stressed to be hungry."

Piers took what was left of her croissant and downed it in one bite. It was basically butter and air. How did a whole people survive on this?

Finished chewing, he wiped his fingers on a red-and-white checkered napkin that matched the tablecloth. A little candle burned in a glass bowl on the table, brightening the afternoon gloom. It reassured him. At least not all the light and heat came from unknown sources.

"Thank you, Sophronia." He could eat ten more, along with a leg of lamb, but he didn't mention that.

"*Please*, call me Sophie. Sophronia is what my mother calls me when she wants to guilt me into doing something I'd rather carve out my left eyeball than do."

Piers chuckled. He didn't know how he could laugh when his life had been turned inside out, and Sophronia —*Sophie*—was in danger, but she made him smile. He liked that. "I'm comforted in the knowledge that mothers are the same the cosmos over."

She quirked a brow. "The cosmos, eh? I guess you really are an alien."

"If that means I'm not from here, then yes."

She leaned forward, whispering, "Are you human?"

Piers pretended to think about it. "The last time I checked, yes."

Her lips twitched. "Not Thor's long-lost brother, then?"

"I don't know this Thor. Where's he from?"

"Asgard."

Dismayed, Piers shook his head. Yet another world he didn't know about? He was starting to think his time in the knowledge temples wasn't well-spent. "I'm afraid I don't know Thor. Is he your friend?"

Sophie laughed. "I don't know him personally. I think you two would get along great, though, if you ever met."

Piers nodded. He was always interested in meeting new people, especially if they weren't out for blood.

"I can't help thinking I'm in Attica," he said. "Nothing else makes sense. Though…that doesn't make sense, either. We all know Attica lost its magic. Unless the tales aren't true."

Sophie blanched. "Did you say Attica?"

The word obviously struck a chord with her. Piers could tell by the way she stopped. "Why? What is it?"

"You don't mean the prison in Upstate New York, do you? The one where they had that horrible riot?"

He shook his head. "Attica isn't a prison. It's a world. Athena's favored world—or that's what we're taught."

She visibly swallowed. "Attica is the region around Athens. It's a big city named after Athena."

Hope jumped in Piers's chest. "Is she there? Is that her main residence? I mean, other than Mount Olympus."

Sophie couldn't have looked more shocked if Hades had just come knocking from the Underworld. "It's halfway around the world," she whispered, "and the Greek gods aren't…real." She trailed off, squeezing her eyes shut. They popped open again, blue fire in a pale face. "Or I *thought* they weren't real until a few days ago. All that's just stories and myths. Ancient history—here." She added *here* as though she couldn't quite believe there was anything *other*. Piers knew better.

"Athena is as real as you and I. It's the people of Attica that forgot her, not the other way around. When Atticans still worshiped the Olympians, the gods remained. And there was magic, not this *technology* you talk about."

Her brows drew together. "Is there a way to contact Athena?"

Wariness stirred inside him. "Why would you want to do that?"

Sophie sat back, failing to look casual when, clearly, that was her misguided aim. She had no reason to pretend with him, and Piers would have to make sure she knew that. "Just say…hypothetically. Is it possible?" she asked.

He didn't know where she was going with this, but he hated to disappoint her, especially with her thunderbolt-to-the-heart gaze so intense on him and her breath trapped inside her lungs. "I've prayed to Athena all my life and never received an answer. But that doesn't mean she isn't listening. She answers those she chooses to."

Sophie grimaced. Her caged exhalation gusted out in a rush. "So how do you make yourself heard?"

From out of nowhere, a surge of dread rose inside Piers. It came with the echo of a chant, indistinct in his mind, but gut-wrenching and awful. Somehow, he knew down to the very marrow of his bones that finding the words and saying them aloud led to heartbreak and loss.

"You pray. The gods come if and when they want." The words scraped past the stranglehold some memory had on his throat. Days of studying… Weeks of searching… But for what?

Whatever he'd discovered could only be bad, considering his visceral reaction to it. His body must remember something his brain didn't. Piers hated that.

He cleared his throat. "Only those they choose to favor ever see or hear from them. Men aren't meant to have a say in it."

Sophie cocked her head. "What about women?"

"*Humans* aren't meant to have a say in it." Piers wasn't sure how, but he knew bending those laws would be bad.

His last, indistinct moments in Thalyria tried to take shape in his mind. They stayed vague and just out of reach, slipping and sliding until he lost them again. He nearly growled in frustration. Why couldn't he remember? What had Cat done to him? Because he had no doubt his brother's hot-headed wife was the one who'd broken his nose and left him bruised and aching. But why? Cat was a self-centered brute, but she'd never attacked him before. So…

What had *he* done?

The question churned like spoiled meat in Piers's stomach. He set it aside for now. From the look on Sophie's face, her troubles were just as bewildering and pressing as his.

"What's going on, Sophie?" He reached for her hand across the table. If he couldn't solve his own problems, maybe he could help Sophronia with hers. "Why this sudden interest in gods you think are pure mythology? They're not, by the way." He had to add it. The urge was too strong. "Tell me what's wrong, so I can try to help." He was beginning to think he was here for that—for her— because nothing else made sense.

Sophie chewed her bottom lip, which Piers tried hard not to find distracting. "It's why those men were chasing me. A friend of mine sent me this ice shard. He works"— she gulped down a quick breath—"*worked* for a completely unhinged billionaire scientist who must've dug it up from somewhere. Maybe Mount Olympus." A distraught laugh tangled in her throat, and she lowered her voice. "My friend said it's super powerful. Or else, it *makes* people powerful. I'm not really sure. He sent it to me because I'm supposedly vaguely related to Heracles, and he somehow thought that meant *I* could give the Shard of Olympus back to Athena. But I can't. I don't know how."

"The Shard of Olympus?" Piers's interest exploded, and he was already interested enough.

"Right?" A harder laugh burst from Sophie. She shook her head. "A few days ago, Athena and the rest of the Olympians were just stories to me, and even if they're real, you don't just dial up a goddess and say, 'Hey girl, come get your shard back.'"

Piers wondered if *dialing up* was the equivalent of praying here. "Can you show it to me?" he asked.

Sophie sliced her head back and forth. "Not here. *It glows*. Those hired guns were calling it a crystal, but I think it's ice that never melts. It's so freaking cold." She shivered from head to toe.

Piers tightened his hold on her hand, instinctively trying to warm her. "I've seen something like this before. My brother Griffin's wife Cat has a necklace made from the same type of ice shard from Mount Olympus. It shores up her already considerable power when it's depleted and amplifies it when it's not."

"Power...as in...magic?" Sophie wrinkled her nose. She didn't *want* to believe. Piers could tell her skepticism wasn't stopping her from starting to accept the truth, though.

He nodded. "I don't think even Cat knows this about her necklace, but I've done some research. Those rare chunks of Olympian glacier that never melt? It seems they've been struck by Zeus's thunderbolt. The intensity of the magic hardens them to rock—crystalizes them, in a way—and infuses them with a small portion of the primordial power the Elder Cyclopes used to forge Zeus's lightning bolt. But magic only works where magic exists. It's strong in Thalyria. Here, it's supposed to be long gone."

"Then what does it mean if there's magic in the ice shard?" Just from her low, trembling question, Piers knew there was—and that Sophie had felt it.

Unfortunately, he wasn't sure. "It must mean it's very

powerful. Maybe from Zeus's first lightning strike. Or..." His nostrils flared. *Could it be?*

"What?" Sophie asked.

"What if your shard goes all the way back to powerful, new magic created not for just one god but for *three*? The Titan War happened here, on Attica. Zeus and his brothers were instrumental in toppling the Titans—Zeus with his lightning bolt, Hades with his invisibility helmet, and—"

"Poseidon with his trident," Sophie finished for him. "What if the shard contains magic from all three gifts from the first Cyclopes?"

Piers was thinking the same thing. And it was a frightening concoction of power. "Then it would truly be *the* Shard of Olympus—one of a kind and made when the brothers stood back-to-back, conquered the Titans, and forged a new kingdom."

"Holy shit." Sophie gaped at him.

"That might explain how it still holds magic after thousands of years in a place with none," Piers said, starting to worry about the lack of color in Sophie's cheeks. "Power like that doesn't fade," he added. "It's just too strong."

"I knew this was bad." Her fingers curled around his, gripping hard. "In the wrong hands, it could be a weapon. A terrible weapon."

Piers squeezed her back. "But yours aren't the wrong hands." He'd seen enough to know that. "The instructions were to give it to Athena?"

She nodded. Her eyes ate up half her face, and a visible swallow tracked down her throat.

"Then that's what we'll do," Piers said.

Sophie nodded again, less hesitant this time. Her expression blared fear, but something else, too. Strength. Determination. A woman who didn't give up without a fight—who maybe didn't give up at all.

Pride welled in him. His Sophronia was a warrior. And suddenly, this world didn't seem so foreign to him. "What do you feel when you touch it?" he asked.

"Cold." She shuddered.

"What else?"

Reluctantly, Sophie added, "A vibration. A kind of constant buzzing, deep down."

Magoi. He knew it. Maybe once she understood her magic, and with the help of the Shard of Olympus, she could send him home.

The thought twisted inside him as though wrapped in thorns, and Piers drew her hand closer across the checkered tablecloth, keeping it tucked in his. "We'll figure this out. If Athena wants that shard off this world, she'll come for it. We just have to make it easy for her."

"You really think so?" Hopeful now, a little breathless, her cheeks gaining some color again, Sophie outshined everything in the room.

Piers could safely say she blinded him, and he was used to the dazzlingly bright Thalyrian sun.

He nodded, his fascination growing by the second. The urge to touch her, comfort her, *protect* her, intensified, and he reached for her other hand as well. Holding them both felt right—righter than the idea of letting them go. "The shard doesn't belong here. Not anymore. It must've been buried. Or forgotten and left behind. If it made its way to *you*, there's a reason the Fates wove it into your life." *Into mine...* "You must be able to connect with it somehow. Or connect to the gods."

"The Fates..." Sophie's brow furrowed, but then she nodded. Something about the idea of destiny seemed to calm her down. "Thank you, Piers of Sinta. Gamma of the realm and third in line for the throne."

Piers wasn't extraordinarily fond of being teased, but if it put a glimmer back in Sophie's blue eyes, he could get used to it. Gruffly, he muttered, "You're welcome."

She grinned. "It seems crazy, but I'm starting to think Athena put you in my path. Or maybe the Fates did."

Piers thought it was likely some combination of both. Athena could just as easily have knocked on Sophie's door and asked for the shard, but the gods didn't work like that. They watched events unfold and set possibilities into motion. Then they saw what came of things, good or bad. There was destiny, and there was free will. It was the sticky, confusing, interlocking mix of both that fascinated the Olympians as they observed, sometimes neglecting, and sometimes nudging, from their mountaintop.

"I'm really glad you're here." Sophie's thumbs swept over his knuckles and back again, her skin silky-soft and warm.

Piers's flesh tingled, his blood heating to her touch. Their eyes met, and his pulse sped up. He couldn't remember the last time he wanted to throw all caution to the wind, wrap his arms around a woman, and kiss her.

Emotion expanded in his chest. He wanted to be the

man Sophie turned to for more than just the Shard of Olympus, and the thought simultaneously elated and terrified him. It pierced his heart and stuck there like a barbed arrow from Eros. She'd become precious to him too quickly for anything other than the Fates to be steering this strange and unexpected course. Then, what happened when he found his way back to Thalyria and his family? What happened if he *didn't*? In both scenarios, he lost.

His gut churned again, tight with worries. Piers was sure of one thing, so he focused on it.

"I want to help you, Sophie." He wouldn't fail her, no matter the cost. "If there's a way to contact Athena, we'll find it. I promise." He might have a sword strapped to his back—and gaining him odd looks from the other restaurant patrons—but he was a researcher and a scholar above all else. He'd investigate; he'd find a solution; he'd do whatever needed to be done. Then Sophie would be safe.

"As insane as all this sounds, I believe you. And I'm not half as scared anymore. Two is stronger than one, and together is way better than alone." Sophie's smile punched Piers right in the chest and left him short of breath.

Sophronia's was a thousand-ship smile, the kind nothing was off-limits to protect. His heart drummed. His world shifted.

So, this was how lightning struck.

"Then consider me your other half," he rasped.

Her smile gained a playfulness he hoped she'd never lose. "I might not be great at math, but don't two halves usually make one?"

Exactly.

Sophie finished her coffee, her spirits brighter than before, and Piers kept watch with new vigilance. The Olympian treasure she had in her possession was no laughing matter, and whoever wanted it would send more soldiers. He'd be ready when they did.

Not long after, Sophie caught the waiter's attention and asked for the bill—apparently, a multipurpose word.

Piers narrowed his eyes. Luckily, he hadn't let her call him *that*. It was almost as bad as Bob.

CHAPTER 4

***"It's just a small detour,"* Sophie insisted, linking her** arm through Piers's and tugging him in the direction of Rockefeller Center.

Man, this guy was stubborn. When he set his mind to something, he was like a donkey with a carrot. Only way hotter. He smelled good now, too. Too good. She kept trying to sniff him, and she wasn't usually a sniffer. Was anyone? She'd have to read up on pheromones. There was definitely something like that at work here. She'd seen a book back home in the window of her local bookshop: *Alchemy and Opposite Sexes, The Mystery of Attraction*. That was what she needed—information. Maybe it would explain why she couldn't stop staring.

"Don't you think we have more important things to do?" Piers grumbled.

Yes, in fact, she did. But she'd been on the run for days, scared out of her mind, and totally alone. Right now, she had company, felt almost safe for the first time since Aaron's package turned her life upside down, and was actually starting to believe there might even be a way out of this mess that didn't involve someone from Novalight Enterprises prying the Shard of Olympus from her cold, dead hand. Sophie needed a break, so she was taking one.

"You'll love it. I swear." Who didn't like a little holiday sparkle? "Christmas is in two days. You've gotta see the tree all lit up."

"Fine. Shiny tree. *Then* the ice shard." Piers gave in, letting Sophie drag him beyond their hotel. He glanced back at the revolving door as if he wanted to give it a whirl. Earlier, he'd gone through one at a department store just for the hell of it. She'd tried really hard not to laugh, especially when he did the whole circle a second time to get a better look at the cheery window displays. That was when she knew they had to do the most touristy thing in New York City in December.

"Good. You won't regret it. I'm not letting you get sucked back to wherever you came from without seeing Rockefeller Center at Christmas." A stab of apprehension tried to dim Sophie's smile. She didn't like the idea of Piers suddenly getting plucked from her life by some unknown force. In half a day, she'd come to rely on him for safety, appreciate his insight, and crave his company. Talk about quick work. Her rational mind had whiplash.

She wasn't sure how—possibly all those paranormal romance novels and fantasy TV shows—but she'd adjusted surprisingly quickly to the idea of Piers being from a different world where they worshipped the gods of Olympus. Aaron's whole *the-Greek-gods-are-REAL* thing probably helped. And the glacial-blue shard *glowed* for her. She'd inspected it from top to bottom, her fingers turning numb, and there was no reason for the chunk of ice to shine, let alone not melt into a puddle. Piers said it was magic, and she believed him.

As to why it glowed for *her*... Apparently, that had something to do with her being *Heracleidae*. It really wasn't such a stretch to accept that she truly descended from Heracles. Herakles to Greeks. Hercules to the modern world. Sophie didn't believe—or rather, *hadn't* believed—a lot of that stuff about him completing his twelve herculean labors and becoming immortal, but she'd always thought he was a real person who'd become famous thanks to a certain number of monumental exploits. Heracles supposedly had sex with the fifty daughters of King Thespius in one night and impregnated every single one of them. They gave him fifty sons, and that was on top of his other children, so it wasn't crazy to think there were Iraklidis all over the place. Maybe they didn't all have the name, like she did, but they were out there. She knew that. Besides, as insane as everything sounded, she didn't feel unhinged. Piers, for all his weirdness, didn't seem unhinged, either. And if they didn't mutually require a psychiatric hospital, then they needed to figure out how to contact Athena and give her the Shard of Olympus.

Okay, that sounded a little crazy. But she was going with it.

Sophie savored the smell of roasting chestnuts and smiled to herself as they walked, light snow falling around them. She wasn't alone in this anymore. The Olympian gods had sent her a guardian angel. She didn't care that she was tragically mixing her religions. It felt right to her. *Piers* felt right. Like destiny.

"Do you think I'll get *sucked back*?" he suddenly asked her. "To Thalyria?"

"I don't know." It was on the tip of Sophie's tongue to say she hoped not, but that would be incredibly selfish. She had no idea what Piers wanted, but it probably wasn't to be stuck on a foreign planet helping a woman he'd only met a few hours ago. She was honest, though, so she added, "If you do, I hope we figure out how to get the ice shard to Athena first. I don't think I can do this on my own." She didn't have the first clue where to start. A trip to the Acropolis? Manhattan was expensive enough. Last-minute tickets to Athens would break her bank account.

The helplessness she'd been feeling for the last several days flared up again, though not quite as bad. At least her family was safe in Pinebury, but she couldn't go back until Novalight knew she didn't have the shard. She couldn't risk her family being used against her. She'd hand that magic icicle over in a New York minute, global consequences be damned. Unfortunately, there was nothing stopping Novalight's hired guns from going to

Pinebury anyway and using her family as leverage. Just because they hadn't done it yet, didn't mean they wouldn't. Which meant she and Piers had to resolve this fast.

Sophie shivered. Piers stopped and pulled up her hood even though she had a hat on. Her heart tumbled. She murmured a thank-you as he gazed down at her, his gray eyes dipping to her mouth. Warmth coiled through her, and her pulse sped up. Sophie's lips parted. She hadn't been kissed since a not-too-tragic date ages ago. The kiss had been utterly uninspiring, and she'd felt so much *nothing* she'd started to wonder if her girl parts were broken. But lack of use apparently hadn't damaged anything. All Piers had to do was look at her like he was thinking about kissing her and a hot thump sprang to life between her legs.

"Sophie." The soft, low rumble of his voice caressed something deep inside her. He brushed a wisp of hair off her face.

Heat shivered down her spine. She swallowed. "Yes."

"Your nose is very red."

She blinked and burst out laughing. "Like Rudolf?"

Piers frowned. "I don't know this Rudolf."

"Well, he has a very red nose. He's also a reindeer, which—before you ask—is an animal with four legs and antlers."

"What makes this animal special? Does it breathe fire? Spit poison saliva? Shoot venomous darts from its tail?"

Her eyebrows crept up. "Wow. Thalyria sounds like fun."

Piers cracked a smile and started walking again. "Well?"

"Okay, I'll give you the scoop on Rudolf." Sophie slipped her arm back through Piers's. She liked it there. "He brings holiday cheer and helps deliver presents to children around the world. He's also totally made up—a myth. And our version of magical, I guess, because he flies and has a glowing red nose. Regular reindeer—feet on the ground, no lightbulb noses—are real, though. They're super cute, but I think they're kind of smelly."

"Have you encountered one?" he asked.

"I've never been up close and personal with a reindeer. I hit a regular deer with my car once, though." It got up and ran away, but she'd been so shaken she'd driven well under the speed limit for days.

Piers's brow drew low. "Were you all right?"

"I was sad. I was scared I hurt it."

"More worried about the animal than yourself..." He seemed thoughtful all of a sudden. "Life *does* have more value here. Killing is so common where I come from. People war, and people die. That's just the way of it."

"It sounds..." *Awful*. "Harsh."

"Maybe it's because the Olympians abandoned this world. You seem to have done better without them."

Sophie winced. "You wouldn't think that if you watched the six o'clock news."

He frowned. "The what?"

"I'll explain later." She squeezed his arm. They'd almost reached the most spectacular winter sight in the city. "Look." She pointed as the massive ice-skating rink and huge Christmas tree came into view. Snow swirled in the air, bells jingled somewhere, and all the bright, colorful lights looked festive and wonderful.

Sophie sighed in happiness. Not *everything* was a mess. This was just as it should be.

"Good gods." Piers stopped and stared. "That's...impressive."

"Right?" Excited, she tugged him closer. Rockefeller Center at Christmas took her breath away, and she'd seen it before, both in person and on television. "It's not magic, like you have where you're from, but I think it's pretty magical."

Nodding, Piers wrapped his arm around her shoulders while he took in the plaza. As one, they inched closer together, eliminating the gap between them. Sophie's heart beat faster. Excitement thrummed inside her. She couldn't imagine so easily touching anyone else, but she looped her arm around Piers's waist and leaned her head against him. She loved how towering he was, how broad, and how freaking warm on a winter afternoon. He was the very definition of tall, dark, and handsome.

She relegated her worries about the shard and everything else to the back burner and just let herself enjoy the closeness, her body a riot of sensations she hadn't felt in forever. And never this strongly. Sophie was starting to think she was going to try to have her wicked, wild way with Piers back at the hotel room, which would probably shock his old-fashionedness into the next world over.

And what would that be? Atlantis? She would've laughed at the thought if she hadn't been so breathless.

It took a huge effort not to turn and jump on Piers, lips first. She'd never trusted someone so completely this quickly. Add to that trust a blood-sizzling attraction, and her girl parts hadn't only woken up; they were clamoring for action.

"It's beautiful. Stunning. Special." Piers hugged her tighter, his jaw pressing against her forehead. Somehow, Sophie knew he meant *her* just as much as Rockefeller Center. Her heart clenched, and the idea of Piers being torn from her life just as quickly and surprisingly as he'd entered it suddenly made her want to hold on to him with all her strength and in any way possible.

Maybe it was the harrowing circumstances. Or maybe that stray thought she'd had about destiny hadn't been just a stray thought. If the Olympian pantheon Piers worshipped had a hand in this, the Fates probably weren't far behind. In fact, they were probably well ahead of everyone.

Sophie breathed Piers in, along with the crisp scents of pine boughs and winter. Mulled cider. Rink ice. Snow and a hint of exhaust. It was New York, after all. Piers's big hand squeezed her shoulder, half comforting and half an erotic zap she felt deep in her belly. She wanted his hands on her. She wanted them everywhere. Her whole body tightened. Luckily, she was good at multitasking, because she'd just added *Seduce Piers* to her immediate agenda.

A red light flashed, distracting her. She glanced down. The little dot stopped on her chest, right over her heart. Her pulse exploded. "Oh my God," Sophie breathed out, her muscles freezing solid.

"What is that?" With his free hand, Piers swiped at the little red spot on her parka. He tried again, scowling.

"Someone's aiming a gun at me." Fear shattered her voice down to a broken whisper. "They're hidden somewhere. A rooftop. A window." Only her eyes moved as she scanned the buildings in front of them, seeing nothing. "They can kill me from a distance."

"Like with an arrow?" Piers's sharp gaze followed hers to the rooftops. His arm tightened around her shoulders.

"A bullet. More powerful than an arrow. Faster." She'd be dead before they even heard the shot go off. A tremor went through her. And here, she'd been feeling almost safe. *Stupid*. She should've stayed out of sight. She should've run to a new city. *Stupid. Stupid.* Panic surged, turning her heart into a sledgehammer.

Something sharp pressed into the small of Sophie's back. Her eyes shot wide, and she sucked in a breath.

"You're almost making this too easy," a rough voice said behind her. "Give me the crystal, and you walk away from here. No mess. No questions. That's what we all want, isn't it?"

Piers dropped his arm from around her shoulders with such a hard downward strike that Sophie heard the knife clatter to the pavement. He yanked her hard at the same time, whirling her away. She dove behind the barrier overlooking the skating rink.

"Piers! Get down!" she shouted. A shot could go off at any second. Why didn't it? Too many people? Too conspicuous? If a shooting in the heart of New York City at

Christmas ever got traced back to Novalight Enterprises, it would ruin a man already disliked by millions.

She glanced anxiously around the plaza. Maybe the gun was just to scare her into cooperating, and the man with the knife was supposed to retrieve the ice shard.

Piers stood between her and Novalight's agent, the laser dot still there and trained on the back of his head now. The sight of it made her stomach flip over. Piers gripped the knife wielder's forearm. He squeezed so hard the man grimaced. A second later, Sophie heard a crack.

The hired gun gasped. "Holy... Fuck!"

"Come after her again, and I'll break your neck instead," Piers growled. He threw her assailant six feet using nothing but one hand and the man's mangled forearm.

Sophie's jaw dropped. People all around them screamed and scattered. She didn't know whether to be impressed or horrified. She decided on impressed. Who needed Thor? She had a freaking gladiator protecting her.

Piers turned to her just as the dreaded shot finally rang out. He winced and grabbed his shoulder.

She lunged for him and pulled him down beside her. "Are you hurt?"

"Not much." He shoved her in front of him and propelled her along the barrier, both of them keeping low as they ran away from the ice rink and melted into the crowd as soon as possible.

"I'm looking at that *not much* back at the room." Her breath came hard and fast, the cold air stinging her lungs as they fled Rockefeller Center.

They should never have left the hotel. First, it was to eat, but she could've ordered room service, even at the exorbitant prices. Holiday sparkle definitely wasn't required for the body to function. Neither were croissants. She'd just wanted one.

Sophie hated herself and her choices as they sped back to their room. She'd decided to play tour guide in the middle of a crisis, and Piers got shot for it. *Shot!* This wasn't a game. And this wasn't her life. Her life was teaching French to semi-motivated high-school students, cooking moussaka with her mother who lived practically next door, and streaming too many TV shows.

"This isn't my life," she said aloud. "It can't be."

Piers slowed at the revolving door to their hotel, pulled her through with him, and dragged her into the lobby. His new jacket had a hole in it. She touched the dark material, finding it hot and wet. *Blood*. Spots swam in Sophie's vision.

"Easy now." Piers swept her into his arms. He kicked the button for the elevator. *Kicked it!* Still holding her, he strode into the first box that opened, elbowed the knob for the twelfth floor, and waited, hardly even breathing hard while she hyperventilated.

"You've been shot," she panted.

"Hmmm."

"*Hmmm?*" Sophie tried to slip out of Piers's arms, but his grip tightened. "We need to go to a hospital!"

"If this hospital is an eating establishment with meat, then I agree. Otherwise, we're going back to the room to look at the Shard of Olympus."

Sophie gaped at him. She'd gaped so much today she feared the expression would freeze on her face, and she'd be gaping forever. "Hospital food sucks," she said as the elevator doors opened.

Piers strode toward their room at the end of the hallway. "Then we'll avoid it. Croissants aren't bad, but I'd need about fifty more of them."

Sophie stared at his strong profile, starting to feel a little less woozy and a little more focused. The man needed protein. She should've known that just from ogling his fit, hard-as-a-rock body. "I'll order room service."

"Will there be cheese?" he asked. "Bread? Lamb?"

"I don't know." She'd been living off coffee and soup—and half a croissant—for days now. "I'll show you the menu."

He nodded. "Choices. Excellent."

"How can you look so normal when you have a bullet in you?" The men she knew would've been squealing in agony. Even her brothers, and they were big and strong —*Heracleidae*, like she was.

But then, she also didn't know anyone who could casually break a man's arm and throw him across the sidewalk. *One handed.*

"It's not in me," Piers said. "It went straight through. I saw it hit the pavement."

"Oh." Sophie swallowed, woozy again. She'd fainted twice in her life, both times at the sight of blood. It was a good thing she wouldn't have to operate.

CHAPTER 5

Piers wanted to look at the Shard of Olympus. Sophie wanted to clean his wound. Since he was apparently incapable of saying *no* to her, he found himself seated on a stool in the brightly lit bathroom getting something called saline solution spewed all over him. It didn't feel good.

"It's nothing," he mumbled. This wasn't the first time something had gone in one side of him and come out the other. It happened. That was war.

As if to echo his thoughts, Sophie murmured, "Jesus, you're covered in scars."

"Piers," he corrected, stung she'd somehow forgotten

his name. That hurt more than this ridiculous little bullet wound.

She paused, then laughed. "I know—Piers. It's like saying *holy shit* or *oh my God*. Honestly, I was taught not to say any of those things, but I slip sometimes. Maybe you have an equivalent from Thalyria I can use. It'll be totally guilt free, which I would *love*."

He thought about it, trying not to get distracted by Sophie's light, delicate touch as she patted his torso dry with a clean towel. "Well, there's *oh my gods*—plural. Everyone uses that, and there's no guilt involved. A friend of mine—Flynn—he likes *Hades, Hera, and Hestia!*"

"That's catchy." Sophie set aside the towel and picked up another bottle from the counter. "Maybe it's the alliteration."

Piers shrugged, immediately regretting it. His wound wasn't terrible, but it was still there and aching.

"Don't move," she scolded. "Now, brace yourself. This might sting." She squirted his shoulder with an ice-cold liquid that nearly sent him flying from the room.

"Zeus's bollocks!" Piers roared. He clenched his teeth. It was all he could do to keep his backside on the stool while the fires of Hades consumed his skin. "What in the Underworld is that?"

"Ooh, I like those. *Zeus's bollocks! What in the Underworld?*" She squirted him again, this time from the back, pushing his hand away when he tried to probe his shoulder. "No touching!"

"What. Is. That?" Piers ground out, breathing hard.

"Antiseptic," she said brightly. "It sterilizes the wound."

"Humph." As much as it hurt—and it did—*now*—Piers couldn't argue with that. His mother and sister—both accomplished healers—were always talking about cleaning open injuries to prevent infection. Besides, anyone with half a brain knew from simple life experience that keeping clean prevented a variety of unsavory conditions. "You could've warned me."

"I did. I said *brace yourself*." She snorted. "Then you started screaming like a baby."

Piers glared at her. "I did no such thing."

"Oh, sorry..." She wasn't sorry at all, the little witch. He narrowed his eyes at her. "You started swearing like a sailor."

"That's better," he said stiffly. "And there's more where that came from."

"I'll bet, Mr. Macho Man."

"*Piers*," he said, exasperated. "It's not that hard."

Grinning, Sophie knelt and patted his torso dry with another clean towel. "Okay, *Piers*. We'll let the bullet wound airdry, but let's wipe off the rest of this. At least it's not bleeding anymore."

Piers glanced at his shoulder. It looked fine. Sure, there was a hole, but it was very small. "I'm sorry I ruined the clothing you gave me."

Sophie scoffed. "Are you kidding? You saved the day. You saved *me*," she added quietly.

Piers saw goose bumps wash down her arms, and the urge to comfort her swelled inside him with the force of a lightning storm. He almost moved but then remembered he was still half dripping with antiseptic.

In a low rasp, he said, "I hope I'm there whenever you need me."

Dipping her head, Sophie finished patting him dry. "I hope you're there even when I don't."

Her soft confession made the muscles in Piers's chest go bowstring tight. A hot twist of longing wrung a hard beat from his heart. Sophie's hair slid forward, brushing his skin. He barely suppressed a groan. He wanted to sink his hands into that thick golden mane and pull her mouth to his.

Gods, she smelled so good. Like wild roses and that soap he'd wanted to lick. Sweet almond and honey—that was it. Two foods he never could resist.

He turned, bringing his nose to the top of Sophie's head. He inhaled deeply, his pulse thudding. His fingers twitched on his thighs, his senses clamoring for more than just sight and smell. He wanted to touch. Taste. He inhaled again, and Sophie went absolutely still. There wasn't a sound in the room except for her breathing. It quickened.

Still kneeling next to him, she tipped her head back. Their gazes met and held. Slowly, Piers reached out and traced the line of her jaw. Sophie leaned into his touch. Then she stretched up and pressed her mouth to his.

The groan he'd been holding back came out like an avalanche. He slid both hands into her hair and pulled her closer, molding his lips to hers. Every time they moved, breathed, Piers deepened the kiss. Sophie opened for him, and his tongue touched hers. She licked him back, a needy little sound purring in her throat. Arousal sizzled down his spine. She was soft, delicious, *on fire*. She blazed to life, and he burned to the ground.

Piers stood, bringing Sophie with him. Her fingers sank into his sides. Her mouth welcomed his. In two steps, he backed her against the wall. Lips fused, hands in her hair, he tilted her head back and kissed her like he'd never kissed anyone in his life—from the very depths of his soul.

A siren shrieked outside, jarring them apart. The sound continued down the avenue, fading quickly, but it broke the spell. Beyond the bathroom, the Shard of Olympus glowed as brightly as an oil lamp in the otherwise dim room, reminding Piers that he needed to protect Sophie, not devour her whole.

She dropped her head back against the wall. "Oh my gods."

He grinned, his blood pumping fast. He couldn't resist another quick kiss and then took her hand, leading her into the larger room.

"No, wait." Sophie pulled him to a stop. "We're not done." She carefully placed two large beige squares over the bullet wound, front and back. They stuck to his skin all by themselves.

Piers contemplated the odd bandages in fascination. They'd gone back out after taking a moment to regroup and obtained their healing supplies at the interestingly named drug store, again using Sophie's little green papers to pay. He could've stayed there for hours exploring the wares and reading the boxes on the shelves, but he'd still been bleeding on and off then, and Sophie had been worried about taking care of him.

He moved his shoulder, finding the ache bearable. Sophie had done a good job, and he told her so.

She shrugged, her already flushed cheeks deepening in color. "I wasn't sure how to explain you at a hospital anyway. I did the best I could."

That was fine by him. If it didn't even serve good food, this hospital was a place to avoid.

"Come," he said. "Let's look at the shard together."

"*Come*," she teased in a deep voice. "You sound very imperious sometimes."

"Is that a bad thing?" Piers was used to giving orders and being obeyed, but he hadn't meant to treat Sophie like one of his soldiers.

She looped her arm through his and moved toward the ice shard. It radiated cold blue light from where it sat on the desk across the room. "It'll be an acquired taste." She glanced up at him with a glitter in her eyes and a smile on her lips. "I might call you Caesar here and there after all."

Piers's heart gave a tight, hard bounce. Did that mean she meant to keep him around and get used to him? Even when all this was over, and she was safe?

He gazed down at the top of her head, feeling something shift in his chest. If he couldn't go home, he'd like that.

What if he *could* go home?

The question hit him like a Cyclops's fist, leaving his head ringing with doubts. Home was home, *family*, and everything he'd ever known and worked for. But lose Sophie? He'd only just met her, but somehow...

Fear sent a hot-cold rush of panic through his veins. His nostrils flared.

Somehow, now that they'd found each other, he knew they weren't meant to be apart.

Sophie gaped at him. Piers liked it.

"I'm supposed to believe that people can do powerful and crazy *magic* with this thing?" She turned a skeptical look on the Shard of Olympus.

Piers nodded. "If you're Magoi, then yes. It'll amplify your natural abilities. Otherwise, it's useless."

"Magoi—a person with magic?"

He nodded again.

"As opposed to Hoi Polloi—the many." Her blue eyes owlishly wide, Sophie reiterated what he'd said earlier. *Hoi Polloi* was a term she'd known anyway. Apparently, people used it the same way here, to describe the general populace.

"In Thalyria, there are many more people without magic than with."

"More Hoi Polloi than Magoi. Got it." She used both hands to sweep her hair back. "But Earth is what you've been calling Attica all this time. No one has magic here. Not *real* magic."

"Are you so sure?" Piers glanced at the Shard of Olympus,

which illuminated Sophie's face with an eerie luminescence. "That doesn't glow for everyone. It didn't glow for me." They'd proved it. Sophie went down the hallway and back to test their theory that the ice shard only shined for her. The moment she'd shut the heavy hotel-room door behind her, the shard went dark. The moment she came back, it lit up again. Being out of the room, she hadn't seen it for herself and didn't want to believe, so they'd documented the experiment on her phone. Piers now knew about a fantastical thing called *videos*, but she still insisted there wasn't magic here. It was absurd.

"You're not only *Heracleidae*; you're Magoi." He was sure.

"Pfffft." She waved her hand in the air.

Piers caught her hand and held on to it. "Think about it. Who was the father of Heracles?"

"Zeus," she said slowly.

"Heracles, the man, died. His immortal side went to Mount Olympus, joining Zeus and the other Olympians. Your lineage isn't only powerful, it's the *most* powerful. You're a direct descendant of Zeus." Just like Griffin's wife, Cat. But while Cat already used her incredible power to conquer realms, Sophie was only just becoming aware of hers. "Any magic that remains in Attica would definitely be trapped inside a person like you."

Her eyes grew rounder. "A person like me?"

Blink. Breathe, Sophie. Piers squeezed the hand he held. "I mean you're special. You're *more*."

Her troubled gaze darted to the glowing blue shard. "But if Novalight can't use the shard for anything, what does it matter if I just give it to him? Then I'll be safe. My family will be safe. I can go home."

"We don't know his origins. Maybe he can."

Sophie chewed her bottom lip, thinking. "I don't think so, which means he's going to eventually figure out that he needs *me* along with the shard."

Piers wanted to crush that possibility under his boot heel and kick it all the way to the Underworld. "Or someone else with a direct ancestral line to a powerful Olympian."

Her face fell. "*That's* what Aaron figured out. That's why he sent me the shard. He knew I could make it work, but Novalight couldn't. But why send it? All that did was put me and everyone else in danger. If it was useless in Novalight's hands, it could've just stayed that way."

"Your friend trusted you to do the right thing with it." Piers pulled Sophie into an embrace he hoped was comforting. She wrapped her arms around his waist and laid her head on his chest, making his heart thud in satisfaction. "If Novalight's as smart and powerful as you say, he'd eventually have discovered how to use the shard to his advantage. You're definitely special, but you can't be the only person in all of Attica with dormant magic. There must be other Magoi. There was just nothing to wake their power like the shard woke yours."

She sighed, her arms tightening around him. "Maybe you're right. I just wish I knew more about it."

"I know one thing. We're lucky the shard ended up in your hands and not in the hands of someone who'd use it for their own gain rather than try to give it back to the gods of Olympus."

"Which we have no idea how to do," she pointed out.

"Understanding your magic might bring us closer."

She sighed again. "Whatever it is just feels like the occasional baby earthquake in my bones."

An image of Cat slid into Piers's mind again. Griffin's wife had never struck him as inherently *bad*, just unbelievably reckless and sometimes selfish. Right now, he'd be willing to humble himself and ask for her help. He was Hoi Polloi to the core and didn't know what magic felt like, let alone how to draw it forth and use it. Cat could teach Sophie everything she needed to know. She could probably even make enough noise to get an Olympian to take notice.

Except she was a world away, and Piers had a feeling he'd done something terribly wrong.

Was Cat all right? Griffin?

Unease ignited under his skin, burning through him like a house on fire. He let go of Sophie and turned away, spearing a hand through his hair. *Gods damn it!* Why was he here? What happened?

The ghost of a word flitted through his mind. *Exile...*

"Piers?" Sophie laid her hand on his uninjured shoulder. "Are you okay?"

He made a gruff sound, shaking his head in frustration. He *hated* being confused. He'd been confused enough for one day. "I can't remember something. Whatever it is will help us. It's important. It's about why I'm here—or how I got here. I think it's all connected—to you, to the ice shard—but there's this...wall between myself and *knowing*. The information's there. I just can't get to it." He hit both fists against his head, trying to jar the knowledge out.

"Stop." Reaching up, she took his hands. "That won't help either of us."

"I think I did something." Voice turning bleak, Piers leaned his forehead against Sophie's. He squeezed his eyes shut. "Something awful."

He could still see them. Griffin and Cat. Kaia. And three shadowy figures he couldn't quite bring into focus. Who were they? Griffin's expression was so damning. If anything, Cat's face showed more sympathy. And Kaia… The fear in his little sister's eyes, the heartache. *His* fault. Piers knew it.

"I must've done something unforgiveable. Something that hurt my family." His throat thickened. "I don't understand. I would *never* hurt my family."

"Maybe you didn't," she whispered.

"No, I did." He was sure of it.

"Okay. Even if you did, that's the past now. Another life. Another *world*." Sophie tipped her head up, bringing her lips so close to Piers's that he could feel them calling to his mouth. Calling to *him*. "You're here now. With me."

"With you?" He swallowed. Maybe he hadn't lost everything. Or maybe he had, but he could start over.

Her eyes flicked up, locking with his. She nodded. Her warm breath swirled against his lips, and Piers's abdomen tightened.

Unable to resist, he anchored one hand on her hip and slid the other around the back of her head. After only a day together, he already couldn't imagine a day apart. "Sophie." Her name sounded so right on his lips.

She gripped his shirt and tugged. That was all the encouragement he needed to claim her mouth for a kiss that turned into a fiery mating dance so fast it incinerated his senses.

Piers clasped her tighter, the heat of her body scorching him through their clothes. Pressure built inside him. His shaft grew heavy and hard. Sophie slid her hands under his shirt, sweeping her fingers over his bare skin. He shuddered in pleasure. He'd never been so aroused.

She broke away, breathing hard. "I can't believe I'm saying this to a man I met this morning, but I want you."

Piers groaned. "Gods, I want you, too." The gift he had in his arms left him reeling, especially when he was sure he didn't deserve such a reward. "You're incredible. Brave and beautiful." He kissed her jaw, her neck, her mouth again. "But there's no rush. I could kiss you for days." He barely knew himself right now. There was no way Sophie could know him. He didn't want her to regret anything, no matter how perfectly their bodies melded together, or how desperately they ached to join.

Wide eyed and beautifully flushed, Sophie huffed a laugh. "No rush? We have Novalight's henchmen after us and a magical ice shard to get rid of. I'm not getting killed tomorrow and missing out on this. On *you*."

"I won't let you get killed." Piers took offense she'd even thought it.

"What if *you* die?" she challenged.

He scoffed. "I've lived this long. I don't plan on dying

tomorrow." Besides, the ruffians here were pathetic. They only stood a chance because of guns.

"That's man-reasoning if I ever heard it." Slowly, she backed toward the enormous bed with pillows for four. "Besides, we're safe for now, alone, and I'm feeling"—she cast about for the right word—"hot." Defiance flared in her eyes, and she dragged her shirt up over her head and tossed it to the floor.

Piers's mouth went dry. Sophie's hair flew in every direction. She smoothed it down as she stood there in her jeans and a bright-pink breast-catching contraption that made his blood roar in his ears. He stared. He could barely breathe, was afraid to move.

She shucked off her socks and jeans, leaving only a tiny pink garment that matched the upper part of her underclothes. He swallowed hard.

Sophie bit her lip, waiting. Piers devoured the sight of her, catching fire from the inside out. He'd never seen anything more erotic in his life than those little pink scraps of clothing—and the magnificent woman underneath.

CHAPTER 6

Sophie's heart beat so fiercely, it pounded her ribs.

Piers stepped closer. "Are you sure?" he rasped in that low, sexy voice of his.

Her belly clenched. That rough hitch... She could *hear* how much he wanted her, and it made putting herself out there in a totally uncharacteristic way surprisingly easy.

"Very." She nodded.

Why wait until tomorrow? A week from now? This strong, capable, selfless, and frankly hot-as-hell man dropped straight into her life today like a penny into a wishing well. She'd needed him, and here he was. The rest was inevitable. Destiny, maybe. All Sophie knew was that she wanted him. And not just for tonight. For as long as possible.

Their kiss still scorched her lips, and the way Piers looked at her sent heat tumbling through her middle. Want pulsed low inside. "You're not going to make me beg, are you?"

He moved so fast he startled her. He lifted her and brought her to the bed, laying her down and settling over her. She brought her knees up. He cradled her head and took her mouth for the most sinfully delicious kiss of Sophie's life. She melted. She wrapped her arms around him and devoured him back, because he was the most delectable thing in the world.

With a ragged sound, Piers broke away and tore his shirt over his head. Sophie saw his bandage and nearly had a heart attack.

"Oh my God, your shoulder!" A big spot of blood stained the bandage.

Ignoring that, Piers pulled off the rest of his clothing. He was totally naked underneath, tanned to perfection, and utterly magnificent. Sophie's mouth almost watered at the sight of him. She'd never seen a flesh-and-blood man who was as impeccably honed and sharply chiseled as a classical Greek sculpture. And wow—that was one hell of an erection.

Her eyes widened. "You didn't figure out the boxers, did you?"

Piers ignored that, too, and leaned back over her, kissing her from jaw to collarbone to the top of her lacey bra. Sophie's breath shuddered. Nuzzling her chest, he dipped his finger under the material, exploring deeper with every stroke. He finally brushed her nipple, and she gasped, heat simmering between her legs.

Piers seemed fascinated by the little details of her lingerie, but Sophie grew impatient when he didn't finish undressing her. She unhooked her bra and tugged off her panties herself. She'd never been so bold or wanton in her life, but with Piers, going full steam ahead not only felt natural; it felt *necessary*.

"I need you," she whispered, arching into his touch.

Roughly, Piers said something in a language that resembled Greek as he smoothed his hand down her body. He stroked and explored as if he had all the time in the world when Sophie had never been so desperate to move faster. She pressed against him, twisting and straining. She needed contact. She needed friction. After breath-stealing minutes of driving her to the brink of insanity, he finally slid his fingers toward her throbbing center.

"Yes." She nearly sobbed in relief at his first light stroke through her hot, aching slickness. "More. There."

Her senses exploded as he touched her. They were just getting started, and this was already the most aroused she'd ever been. Sensation raced like liquid fire beneath her skin. Piers pressed on just the right spot, and it was like hitting a reset button. She moaned in pleasure. Her sex life started now, she decided—with Piers. She grinned at the idea.

"Is my lovemaking funny?" he growled against her neck. His deep voice resonated inside her. "Do they do it differently in Attica?"

"Are you kidding?" she panted. Piers was acing this. "I think they do it wrong here. Don't stop. I love it."

He paused, maybe surprised by her candor. Then he started working the little bead of her clitoris that even *she* had trouble finding. Sophie nearly flew off the bed, which might've been funny if she hadn't been so intensely absorbed in chasing what was sure to be the best orgasm of her life. Piers slid his mouth over her breast and sucked on her nipple. His tongue lashed the tip, and she let out a sharp breath, tension peaking inside her.

She gripped his head, sinking her fingers into his hair and holding on as if her life depended on it. Maybe it did. If Piers didn't make love to her right now, she would implode. She was sure of it.

"Wait," she gasped.

He drew back without question. Voice thick with desire, he asked, "What is it?" He scanned the room for danger.

"Nothing bad," Sophie said. "I've got protection." She always carried a few condoms in her purse and made sure they weren't expired. It had seemed like a pretty useless precaution until several incredibly hot minutes ago. "I'm sure you have ways of preventing pregnancy in Thalyria. This is our method." She leaned over the side of the bed and fished around in her handbag for a little foil package. She finally found one, tore it open, and reached for him.

Piers sucked in a breath when she touched him. His big shaft pulsed in her hand. An answering throb thumped deep in Sophie's belly. She stroked him, the condom in her other hand, watching his gray eyes drift closed and his jaw tighten. She smiled, feeling sexy and powerful as his throat moved on a hard swallow. Piers made her feel like a goddess in the bedroom. It changed everything.

She stroked him harder and licked his lower lip, coaxing him to open his mouth for her. The moment he did, she kissed him fiercely. Possessively. She'd never felt anything but awkward and bored during intimacy. This was so far from awkward and boring that she knew she could never go back. It was this man or nothing.

Piers's breathing turned sharp and uneven. "*Sophronia mou.*" That, she understood. *My Sophronia*. Oh, yes—she was his and then some.

She fumbled with the condom.

Piers took it from her unsteady hands. He covered himself, understanding everything that needed understanding, including that she was no expert at putting it on him. "A sheath but different. Like a second skin."

"That's the idea," she murmured.

He gave himself a long, slow stroke, his arm and shoulder muscles rippling. Heat washed through her, and the raw, needy sound that poured from her throat could've come from a porn star.

Piers clasped the back of her head and drew her in for a kiss that branded her soul. Desperate to feel him inside her, Sophie nudged him onto his back and straddled him. She didn't want any weight on his shoulder. She kissed his rock-solid chest and worked her way up to his mouth again. His sounds of desire came hard against her lips. He gripped her hips and kissed her back, sometimes gently and sometimes like he wanted to eat her alive. It was incredible.

Slowly, she rose up and then sank down on him. Fully joined, she could feel every inch of him inside her, and for one breathless second, they both went still, savoring the sensation. Then she started moving.

Piers slowly exhaled. His eyes grew heavy-lidded. He watched her from under a gleaming, pleasure-hooded gaze, touching her breasts as she slid on him. He tugged on her nipples, lightly at first and then with a hint of roughness that brought Sophie to the brink of orgasm. She held off, keeping the hot pulse from exploding inside her too quickly. Piers took over rocking her. He threw his head back, eyes closed, lips parted, chest rising and falling. The fire-bright pressure mounted. His grip tightened, and he pulled her hard against him. Sophie gasped. She clenched all over, and release pounded through her. Piers joined her with a groan, his hard throbbing adding to her pleasure.

"Wow," she murmured. Breathing as if she'd just run a marathon, Sophie sank down against his chest and nestled her forehead into his neck, careful of his shoulder. She kept making little noises she couldn't seem to control and didn't want to. She couldn't stop kissing him. Chest. Neck. Jaw. Mouth. Piers wrapped his arms around her.

"*Sophronia mou.*" He sighed her name this time, a low, satisfied rumble.

She smiled. She didn't mind when Piers used her full name, and the way he rolled the *r* made her shiver.

They stayed all tangled up in each other for a long time, the room dark except for the city light streaming in through the window and the eerie blue glow of the Shard of Olympus. Piers's stomach eventually growled.

"I'll order room service." Sophie tried to motivate her muscles to move. They felt like jelly.

"Meat," Piers said.

She grinned, reaching for the menu. "You got it."

CHAPTER 7

Piers had two words to describe Sophie. Incredible. Terrifying. Her idea to visit a museum filled with works from what she called "Classical Antiquity" and find sculptures of ancient Greek gods, especially Athena, seemed solid. A good place to start, anyway. If nothing about the ice shard's behavior or any of the statues gave them a hint as to how to return the shard to an Olympian, they'd try a museum with more modern interpretations of Greek mythology.

He shook his head. What he called reality, she called mythology. What he called every-day life, she called ancient civilization. It was enough to make a man feel old and senile.

And what manner of idiot had decided to call important houses of knowledge Met and MoMA? They sounded like names you'd give pets, not places.

At least Sophie had a plan, which was more than what Piers had. But the idea of her being exposed and vulnerable on city streets and in public places made him feel as if he were trying to breathe underwater. It was funny—no, *frightening*—how a single day could change his entire existence. And he wasn't even talking about the inexplicable world-hopping. He meant Sophie.

Piers got it now. Why Griffin would choose Cat over anything. Why Carver lost himself when he lost Konstantina. He was just like his brothers. The right woman hit them like a lightning bolt and scorched herself down to their very essence. Sophie was his lightning strike. He had no doubt the Fates had thrust them together to keep the Shard of Olympus out of the wrong hands. And now that their life threads were weaving the same tapestry, he was going to make damn sure they didn't get cut short or unravel.

Which made Sophie's reckless running around New York City almost unbearable. He grumbled about it again, scanning the surprisingly vast wilderness in the heart of the city for signs of danger.

Sophie sipped coffee from a cup made of paper, his protests rolling right off her. "I haven't been to the Met since I was a kid. I can't wait to see the Greek sculptures again."

"Why Greek instead of Attican?" Piers asked. "Isn't that where they're from?"

She shrugged. "Back then—and now—Attica was just one region around Athens. Ancient Greek civilization spread all over the Mediterranean. It was made up of independent city states that shared a similar culture and language."

"And gods."

"And gods." She nodded.

Piers understood and could even picture what she meant, just as he understood more about this world by the minute. He now knew that Sophie could show him a detailed map of ancient Greece with a few taps of her finger. At the time, it seemed the people there had called their land Hellas.

Why stories of the Hellenes and their ancient kingdoms came to Thalyria as tales from Attica, he could only guess. Perhaps Athena had liked her glorious role as the patron goddess of the area and spread to Thalyria only the information she liked best.

Sophie's phone fascinated him. He could understand why the little rectangles were glued to everyone's fingertips. They'd used hers several times today already. They could buy entrance tickets to this Met. They could check the incoming weather. They could listen to music—if one could call the odd *thump thumping* and endless *la la laing* music. She could even contact her family, her thumbs flying over little letters, to say she'd try to be home soon and not to open the door to any strangers.

Piers wished he had a magic rectangle. But there was

no contacting *his* family with Sophie's phone, no matter how powerful the tool seemed to him.

A horse and carriage rolled by. At least that was something familiar, although he preferred a fast two-wheeled chariot if he wasn't riding. Bells jingled from the harness, and the horse's breath steamed the air. The driver had dressed himself as one of these jolly, red-robed men with big white beards Piers kept seeing everywhere. Sophie said they were Santa and related to the upcoming holiday, although he still hadn't grasped why they were *all* Santa or why one city needed so many of them.

The horse and carriage trundled away, and Piers rubbed his hands together, feeling nostalgic for his home, his horse, and his warm weather. *Good gods*, it was cold here.

"The Met." Sophie pointed to a huge columned building. It looked a lot like Castle Sinta.

Piers stared at it. It was far bigger than any knowledge temple he'd ever been to. "Do they only have these buildings in New York City?" he asked.

She arched her brows. "Well, there's nothing quite this grand in Connecticut."

Ah. Her homeland. "Could I maybe…visit this *Cunnetakit* with you?" It was a bold question, and worry tightened his lungs. What if Sophie said no? What if for her, this, *they*, were only temporary?

A frown slid over her expression. "I would never just abandon you in the city."

Piers nodded, but there was a difference between abandoning someone and bringing a man into your life as a partner. A lover. He decided not to press. It was good enough for now that Sophie planned on keeping him by her side. He'd convince her of *forever* later.

She flashed her phone to gain them entrance to the Met, and they went through a security scan. She'd warned him to leave his weapons at the room, which Piers had wholeheartedly resisted. He understood better now. He'd have been forced to give them up anyway, and Sophie had been worried his sword and daggers looked so "authentic" that the museum might ask questions they couldn't answer.

As they strode through the classical rooms, Piers had to admit, if only to himself, that he hated it. Here was absolute proof that his gods had been abandoned. Left to rot, fall apart, and be scattered throughout museums for people to gawk at without even an inkling of the power the Olympians still wielded across the cosmos. At least the marblework was appealing when it wasn't disintegrating. These statues were the first things to truly remind him of home—but only to prove just how very far away he was.

"Any difference in the shard?" he asked as they stared at yet another rendition of Athena. This one had a hand missing. And half a nose.

Sophie discreetly pulled up her sleeve. She'd fashioned a bracelet to hold the shard out of some thin wire she'd had in her car—leftovers from a school project to build a model of the Eiffel Tower, whatever that was. She shook her head. "It feels the same. Glows the same. Pulses the same. It's still really cold."

"And inside you? Is there a vibration? A call?"

She let her sleeve drop back over the bracelet. "Nothing—or nothing *new*. It's the same as before. Just a weird buzzing in my bones. I know it sounds ridiculous."

"That's the magic inside you, ready to use."

She scoffed. "Use *how*?"

"To defend yourself." Piers glanced back and forth between Sophie and the statue of Athena. "To contact her?"

"Yeah, that's not really working out so far."

No. They'd both tried talking to Athena and the other Olympians as they gazed upon their marble likenesses. They'd muttered prayers, internally and aloud, and even discreetly touched the ice shard to the statues, even though ropes were meant to keep them away. They'd been shushed and scolded by museumgoers several times, and frankly, Piers was losing hope that this would help them. He thought they needed to pray in a temple specifically dedicated to Athena, but Sophie said the most important one was half the world away, in ruins, impossible to actually stand in, and too expensive to get to anyway.

His hands fell to his hips. He pursed his lips. "Should we try your MoMA?" They'd covered the Met's classical sections twice now—Greek and Roman. Apparently, these Romans had come along and adopted his gods but given them different names. Didn't that just confuse people?

"I guess so." Sophie rubbed her fingers over the Shard of Olympus through her clothing. "I'm not sure we're on the right track, though."

Piers leaned in and kissed the top of her head, her

sweet-smelling shampoo making his mouth water. "It's all right, *kardoula mou*. We'll figure it out."

"Sweetheart?" She smiled. "That's nice."

"You understand?" he asked in surprise.

She nodded. "We still use some of the same terms of endearment in my family. I guess that somehow trickled down from our common heritage."

Emotion pushed at Piers's ribs. He liked the idea of them having something in common. It made him feel less lost.

"Come." He squeezed Sophie's hand, holding on to it. "To MoMA."

"To MoMA," she echoed in a soldier's voice.

They were outside and in a quiet, tree-covered section of the park when Novalight himself stepped into their path. Piers recognized him from seeing pictures on Sophie's phone. Self-importance rolled off him like the stench of dung. Several of his hired ruffians flanked him.

"I'd like my crystal now." Voice flat, eyes flatter, Novalight clearly thought he'd get what he wanted now that he'd deigned to show up himself.

"What crystal?" Sophie asked. "Who are you?" She was a surprisingly good actress. Piers doubted anyone but he heard the slight reediness in her voice or noticed how her eyes dilated.

"*My* crystal." Novalight held up a hand to keep his

guards in place when they started forward. "Don't play stupid, Ms. Iraklidis. We both know you're not."

"Fine." Sophie's chin notched up. "How did you find me?"

"I have endless resources, and you're not exactly the queen of stealth." Tall and easily in his fourth decade, Novalight looked as if he might put up a decent fight. Thick jowls gave him a heavy-set appearance, but Piers wasn't fooled. There was at least some muscle beneath that bulk.

Sophie stared Novalight down. A small tremor jumped from her fingers to Piers's, and he tightened his grip on her hand. "It's not yours," she said.

"It *is* mine. I found it. I own an archeological site on a Mediterranean island that's coming closer and closer to being declared the lost city of Atlantis."

Piers scoffed. Atlantis wasn't lost. It was another world—like this one.

Novalight swung an annoyed look on him. "Do you have something to add?"

"More of a question," Piers said. "What do you plan to do with it?"

"Study it. Reveal its potential. Use it." It was impossible to miss the power-hungry gleam in Novalight's eyes. He obviously knew the shard was important, but Piers doubted the man would know magic if it kicked him in the forehead. He must believe the shard could unlock some other prize.

"For what?" Sophie demanded.

"For whatever I deem necessary."

"Spoken like a true psychopath," she muttered.

"I've had just about enough of you, young woman." Novalight's expression hardened. Piers figured the man had been trying to seem non-threatening up until then, but Novalight dropped the act faster than Icarus fell from the sky. "I thought you'd get scared and give up, but then this guy showed up and put me in a difficult position. I'm not a bad person. I don't *want* to hurt you."

"So don't." Sophie hid it well, but Piers felt her shudder.

Rage ignited inside him. How dare this asshole threaten Sophie?

He released her hand, preparing for battle. Novalight might not be the type to get his own hands dirty, but Piers had no problem with bloody knuckles, especially if the blood was Novalight's.

"Then *give me* what's *mine*." The scientist was done playing. That was clear to everyone.

"You killed my friend." Sophie sucked in a breath. Tears gleamed in her eyes.

Piers curled his hands into fists. Did Novalight think several-to-one odds intimidated him? Because they didn't.

"Your friend stole from me and put you in danger. That's no friend." The scientist extended his hand. "Now, give it to me."

"I threw it in the East River. I don't have it," Sophie said.

Novalight huffed. "I trailed you through the museum. I saw it, and I want to know why it glows now." Understanding happened fast. Sophie was right; the man was intelligent, and the calculating look Novalight swept over

Sophie turned Piers's blood cold. "It glows for *you*, doesn't it? Your friend must've known something about you that I don't. Or something about the crystal." His voice turned silky, eager. "I guess we'll find out together, won't we?"

Sophie made a quiet sound of distress. Piers let out a growl. He took a menacing step.

Two of Novalight's guards pushed back their jackets and flashed their guns. Piers stopped. Guns didn't make for a fair fight, and Sophie could get caught in the crossfire.

His nostrils flared. No sword. No knives. A wounded shoulder. He tipped his head toward Sophie, whispering under his breath, "Now would be a good time to figure out your magic."

Her frightened gaze flicked to his. "What?"

"Call it up. See what happens."

Her eyes widened. Piers usually enjoyed her shocked and bewildered expression, but right now, she just looked scared. Scared wasn't cute, and he flat-out despised this Novalight for scaring Sophie.

"Come quietly," Novalight said, "and I'll have no reason to go back to Pinebury."

Sophie froze solid. "What?"

"Such a lovely woman, your mother. Makes a mean baklava. And your father, the renowned architect, is overseeing one of the biggest projects in Connecticut. I hope the ceiling is solid on that new building he's working on. It would be a shame for a freak accident to sully his illustrious career so close to retirement. Or worse, kill someone."

Sophie's voice turned low and seismic. "Leave my family alone."

Novalight's menacing smirk intensified. "Now, Xanthe... She's a treat. Enjoying college for now, her whole life ahead of her. So much potential. Don't you think? But campuses—they can be dangerous. Drunken frat boys... Pathways covered in ice... Rogue delivery trucks..."

Terror twisted Sophie's face. She scuffed back a step, a near-silent "No" leaking from her lips.

Shielding her with his body, Piers bared his teeth at the scientist. "Back. Away," he ground out.

"And you'll make me do that how?" Novalight asked scathingly.

Piers moved fast enough to surprise everyone. He jumped on Novalight like an animal and showed him exactly how savage he could be when his mate was in danger.

Novalight went down hard on his back. Piers followed, pinning him in the cold grass beside the sidewalk. He got in three skin-splitting punches before Novalight's men yanked him backward and threw him down. Their mistake was letting go. Piers surged to his feet and charged the guards, yelling at Sophie to run.

He smashed two heads together. The men crumpled. Someone hit him in the back of the skull with something hard. Piers dropped to one knee, his vision darkening. He spun on instinct with one leg out and knocked over the person behind him. He blinked hard, his head ringing. Lurching up, he punched the blond he recognized from the day before. The blond staggered. Novalight started to stand. Piers grabbed a midsized female before she could free her gun from its holster and tossed her into Novalight, toppling him again.

"Piers!"

He whirled. They had Sophie. Fear tore through his chest.

One man gripped her from behind while another tried to rip the shard from her wrist. Sophie twisted, kicking out, and a third darted in and punched her in the face. She blanched.

"Soph!" Dread gripped his throat.

She sagged, but her eyes lifted, meeting his. Then she lit up like a torch. Lightning cracked from her body and sent the three men flying off. She reeled in shock. The last two ruffians charged, including the blond. She held up her hands to ward them off and twin thunderbolts shot from her palms.

She gasped. So did Piers. She'd laid out five men. They smoldered on the sidewalk.

Sophie looked at her hands in horror. "Oh my God."

Novalight shoved the female soldier aside and crouched. The woman scrambled to her feet and ran. With his power-fevered eyes avidly trained on Sophie, the scientist didn't even see Piers's boot coming for his head. Piers knocked him unconscious and raced to Sophie's side.

He grabbed her still-hot hand and pulled her from the scene of the fight. A family out for a walk had just stumbled upon their secluded pathway, and the mother lifted her phone just as he and Sophie ducked into the woods.

They ran until their lungs burned. They ran until they

left the park. They ran all the way back to their hotel room. They ran until Sophie collapsed on their bed.

"I killed people. I killed people. I'm going to jail." She turned and sobbed into his chest. The lightning in her blood—the most incredible and rare of all magic—had long since sunk back inward, leaving her cold to the touch.

Piers gathered her close, trying to warm away her shock. He rocked her as she cried, telling her again and again that she hadn't killed anyone. He'd looked, and he was sure. Novalight and his henchmen were all alive—which meant they weren't done yet.

CHAPTER 8

Sophie thought she was scared before? This was worse.
Her hands had lit up and *electrocuted* people. Her entire body had become a high-voltage *weapon*. She'd thrown a bunch of men off her with only the *intention* of defending herself. She'd made *lightning*.

She kept trying to wrap her head around the idea, but apparently, her mind wasn't that bendy. Nothing made sense to her. Except for fear. There was plenty of that.

According to Piers, lightning wielders only came from Zeus's bloodline. And the magic only manifested in the most powerful and unique of people. His brother's wife, Cat, was apparently one of these mega-special Magoi, and she was practically a demigoddess on her way to ruling an entire continent!

What a special snowflake.

Evidently, so was Sophie. A special snowflake. Alone on Earth. Able to zap people.

"Oh my God," she murmured for the five hundredth time in an hour.

"*Gods*." Piers squeezed her shoulder with strong, reassuring fingers, stopping her manic pacing. "I think it's time to start believing."

Oh, she believed, all right. She believed she needed to get the hell away from that ice shard and go back to Connecticut. She loved Pinebury. She loved teaching. She loved her family. She did *not* love the Shard of Olympus. "We have to get rid of that thing."

"You might lose your magic. The shard might be the only thing giving you access to it here in Att…on Earth," he said.

"Good." Sophie glared at the shard on the desk, backing away from it. "I want it gone forever."

"Are you sure?" Piers frowned in thought. "You—and the Shard of Olympus—could be the key to bringing magic back to this world."

Possibly the most inelegant sound she'd ever made shot from Sophie's mouth. "That's the last thing this world needs. People are already destructive enough without adding unstoppable superhero powers to the mix." She huffed, shaking her head. "You can't tell me everyone in Thalyria uses their magic for good. Even your sister-in-law,

Cat. You keep saying she's a reckless, power-hungry warmonger. And she's your *family*!"

Piers's lip curled. "She's Griffin's wife. Not my family."

That sounded like the same thing to Sophie. "You don't always get to choose, Piers. Sometimes, it's someone else's choice, and if you love that person, you just have to accept it."

A shadow flitted through his eyes. He pinched his forehead. He looked guilty as hell, but Sophie didn't have the emotional capacity right now to deal with whatever troubled him. She had her own epic freak-out going on. "And besides—"

"What's that?" Piers pointed at the television.

Sophie glanced over. They'd turned on a local news station to try to see if there was, you know, a *manhunt* going on for them. She half expected to see Novalight hopping up and down and proclaiming himself a victim, but it was only an advertisement for tours to the Statue of Liberty and Ellis Island.

"The Statue of Liberty." She waved a hand toward the screen, distractedly explaining, "It's a symbol of freedom and hope to anyone seeking a new home or refuge in this country. Kind of like you, I guess."

"It's Eleutheria. It's a colossus of Eleutheria. She personifies Liberty."

"You mean Libertas? Oh, wait…" Sophie watched the images scroll by on the muted television. "Eleutheria must be the Greek equivalent. Libertas is the Roman goddess they used as a model."

Piers stared at the screen as if he didn't even hear her. "*Zeus Eleutherios*," he murmured. "Protector of freedom."

Sophie's heart started to pound. "Is that where we need to go? Should we bring the shard to the Statue of Liberty?"

Aaron's cryptic message had been burned into her mind since the second she put all those torn-up pieces of paper together. She saw it again.

The Greek gods are REAL. Contact Athena and GIVE THE SHARD BACK TO THE GODS OF OLYMPUS.

Sophie glanced at the glowing ice shard. She swallowed. At first, she'd just wanted to avoid getting caught and losing the shard to a murderous megalomaniac like Novalight. Then Piers showed up, and the whole *Contact Athena* thing went from pure fantasy to possible reality. Same with *magic*. Now, he was staring at the screen in utter shock, as though the Statue of Liberty were just the temple they needed to finally contact the gods.

Or maybe it was something else?

"Piers?" He had a really weird look on his face.

The news channel switched to an advertisement for car insurance, Lady Liberty disappeared, and Piers lost it. No, he didn't just lose it. He lost it like a boss, grabbing his head, curling in on himself, and *howling*.

Sophie froze in shock. Her own massive freak-out took a backseat to Piers's sudden breakdown. She watched, her jaw sliding loose as he wrapped his arms around his head and rocked, groaning and muttering names she knew from hearing him talk about his family. Griffin. Kaia. Cat.

Fear jackknifed through her. She reached for him. "Piers? What is it?"

He abruptly stood and brushed her off. Pale as snow before it hit the New York sidewalk, he turned away from her. Sophie's heart clenched. Something was seriously wrong with him. She tried again, reaching out, and he strode to the bathroom and closed the door. A second later, she heard a huge crash.

She flew to the door, knocking. "Piers? What happened?"

A second huge crash and a bellow.

Jesus. Her pulse throbbed in her ears. "I'm coming in there." She turned the handle. It didn't budge. "If you break it, you pay for it, so *stop* before I can't afford clothes for either of us."

Total silence, then the door flew open. He stood there, his hair in disarray, his chest heaving. Sophie glanced behind him. He'd shattered both big glass panels to the shower. There wasn't any blood on him, so maybe he'd kicked them. The chrome towel rack caught her eye amid the wreckage. He'd ripped the bar from the wall and bent it. How freaking strong was he?

"Holy shit." Sophie snapped her mouth shut. She wanted to be angry at Piers for going all caveman on the hotel bathroom, but he looked so devastated. Beyond devastated—*wrecked*. His eyes glistened, and her heart broke for him without even knowing what happened. She stepped closer and wrapped her arms around him.

Piers stood there for the longest time, stiff and unmoving. Finally, he gripped her back and ducked his head into her neck, holding on as though she were his lifeline. "It's all my fault," he whispered.

She tried to comfort him, smoothing her hands through his hair. She kissed his temple, his forehead. "Whatever it is, we'll figure it out. Just tell me what happened."

"There's nothing to figure out. I made a huge mistake, and now I'm paying for it. I'm here forever. In exile."

The dull monotone of his voice scared her. His will to live seemed to have blinked off faster than a bum string of Christmas lights. At the same time, *here forever* didn't sound that awful to her. It was too selfish to say aloud, but she didn't want to lose him, even if it meant he couldn't go back to his family.

"And you suddenly remembered?" She pulled back enough to look at him. "What just happened?"

"It was your colossus of Eleutheria. Libertas." The Roman equivalent didn't roll off his tongue as easily. "It all came roaring back. Athena said I wouldn't remember at first—that something would trigger my memory when the time was right." His voice turned rough. "That time is now, I guess."

"*Athena* said?" Sophie was getting good at suspending disbelief, but...*Athena?* "Well, that's good, right? We need her."

Piers speared a hand through his hair and started pacing. "No, it's not good at all. I tried to get Cat exiled from Thalyria to keep her from bringing more danger to my family. I didn't want her dead, just gone—*permanently* gone—and she's always picking fights and getting into battles, so I stupidly thought I'd give her a taste of her own medicine and turn her over to Ares, the god of war. I managed to get his attention, which was a colossal error. He would definitely take someone away with him, just not Cat. I didn't count on how strongly the gods favor her, the plans they have. Three Olympians showed up and debated who to seize in Cat's place. Ares threatened to take Kaia—to take my little sister away forever and throw her into endless wars—so I did the only thing I could think of to fix the mess I'd made. I offered myself instead."

Sophie swallowed hard. Of course, he did. She wasn't surprised at all.

"And Cat... She forgave me. Griffin didn't. He won't." Piers's voice rasped hard. He cleared his throat. "Ares could've taken any of us—whoever he wanted. I could've doomed my brother or my little sister to eternal war, but Athena stepped in and argued that I could be useful here, in her world."

"You've been useful to me," Sophie whispered.

Piers prowled back to her, his gray eyes two pain-filled thunderclouds. She'd almost stopped noticing his slightly swollen nose and scraped chin, the scratches on his arms...

"Did you fight with Griffin?" she asked, gently touching his jaw.

"With Cat. She could've killed me. She didn't."

"Maybe she's not so awful, then?"

"*I'm* the awful one," Piers bit out. "I tried to control forces I didn't know enough about and nearly ripped my family apart. As it is"—he laughed harshly—"I'm the only one who got torn from everything. From everyone."

"Does your family know what happened to you?"

"They know Athena took me to Attica. She said she had scientists 'running amok with sensitive information,' and that I might be of help."

"So they know you're gone? Forever? They must be devastated." Tears burned her eyes. She'd only known Piers for two days and already knew his family was everything to him. She imagined the devotion went both ways. How could it not? Terrible families didn't make a person like him—loyal, kind, caring. Everything she'd always wanted in a man.

He shrugged, then shook his head. "I'm dead to Griffin. I know that. Cat's pregnant." He swallowed. "I didn't know *that*, but my actions could've taken his wife and child from him in the blink of an eye. *I* did that. I just did."

Sophie reached for him again, but Piers avoided her. The look on his face said he was toxic, and she'd better stay away or get contaminated. She wasn't having it. She planted herself in front of him and stopped him with both hands on his chest. His torso shuddered. "Tell me. What happened."

His face twisted. But instead of shrugging her off, he stayed where he was and put his hands over hers, holding them. "I never liked Cat. She's hot-headed, a know-it-all, and always needs to be the center of attention. I could deal with all that. I mean, she wasn't *my* fated woman, so I was just going to grin and bear it for Griffin's sake, but then she started dragging my family—my friends, too—into extraordinarily dangerous situations. Quests nearly to Mount Olympus. Arena games to the *death*. Trying to overthrow enemy royals in their own throne room." His mouth went flat. "My sister Jocasta ended up in the middle of it. My brother Carver almost died. Griffin was in constant danger…"

"So, you thought if Cat was out of the picture, all that would stop?"

He nodded. "But it wasn't her. It was Griffin. Cat was the weapon—and the emblem. But he was the driving force. That was the partnership the gods decided for them. *Griffin* pushed Cat toward her destiny. I didn't see it until that last moment. Never truly saw *her*… or her worth."

Softly, Sophie asked, "Do you regret what you did?"

He squeezed his eyes shut. "More than you can imagine."

She tried not to let his words cut like a knife. This wasn't about her. Piers could never say he was sorry to his brother. Never make amends with Cat. Never see his little niece or nephew. Never see his family again. "I'm so sorry." She leaned into him, offering her arms as comfort.

"You're not to blame. I am."

Throat thick, she said, "That doesn't mean my heart can't ache for you."

Piers wrapped his arms around her, holding her tight. His voice dropped to a whisper. "Thank you."

As they stood there, Sophie wondered if Piers really believed in fated mates, and if things like that really happened. Because that would explain how she'd fallen in love with him so quickly. A lightning-bolt attraction—no pun intended—and the unusual situation probably made everything more intense, but somehow, she *knew*. Piers was it for her.

"There is some good news," he murmured. "What I did to get exiled? It was a summoning chant. I know how to call an Olympian. I can compel Athena to us here, right now. That must be why she pushed us together."

Sophie's eyes shot wide. She tilted her head back, looking at him. "Really? That's amazing! That's perfect!" Her gaze darted to the shard. She could get rid of that glowing bit of Olympian ice and get back to her safe, *sane* life just in time for Christmas!

So why did Piers's expression say it was anything but amazing? He looked as though he'd swallowed a razor blade, and it was cutting him in half.

"Piers?" A terrible feeling sank through her.

"Call a god, lose a soul. You see, I figured out just enough to know that summoning an Olympian could be a means to exile. I didn't understand that the summoner doesn't get to choose who goes. Someone's permanent exile is the *result* of calling on a god for a favor. It's not supposed to be the favor itself." His eyes darkened and locked with hers. "Athena will come when I call, but she'll rip us apart. That's the price we'll pay for using magic that's supposed to be long lost. That's the price to pay for summoning a god."

CHAPTER 9

Sophie stumbled back, and Piers's lungs tightened. His punishment was just beginning, wasn't it? He knew he'd been an asshole to Cat and deserved to suffer, but if the gods' goal was to finish him off, they were on the right track. He'd already lost his home and family. He didn't think he'd survive losing Sophie.

"Rip us apart?" She scraped her hair back with shaking fingers. "You mean…take one of us away? Exile?"

"Those are the rules." Piers barely recognized his voice. His words hitched on the lump in his throat. "And we don't get to choose who goes, although I'll offer myself and hope she takes me."

"No!" Then Sophie winced, her face washing of color.

Piers shook his head. "Not you, *Sophronia mou*. You have everything here. I have nothing."

"You have me." The tremor in her voice nearly undid him. Piers's heart folded in on itself.

Having Sophie was precisely the problem. She was *all* he had. And the summoning chant meant losing a soul close to him. Piers hadn't understood that part of the old texts until it was too late, and Kaia, especially, ended up in grave danger. He'd offered himself instead, and the gods had accepted. They might not accept again.

"You should be far away from me when I summon her. Distance might help, although I'm not certain. I'll give the shard back."

"Why wouldn't distance help?" Sophie's blue eyes ate up half her face. So scared. So beautiful. So *his*.

A chasm cracked down his chest. *Why?* Punishing him shouldn't mean punishing Sophie. Later, he would rail against the Fates, but right now, he could sacrifice without question as long as she was safe.

"The price is a soul close to me." That likely meant someone he cared about, but it could maybe simply mean a person in the room.

Her breath shuddered out. Piers would give anything to comfort her. He even thought there might be a small chance at a way for them to stay together, but he refused to get her hopes up. And maybe his own.

He glanced at her phone. He'd have to make a call before he started chanting. He'd have to time it well.

"Why would this happen? Any of it?" Sophie abruptly sat on the edge of the bed. Her fingers curled into the blanket. "If the gods are all-powerful and everywhere, why not just pluck the shard from Novalight's people in the Mediterranean? Or from Aaron? Athena could've just knocked on my door in Pinebury and asked for her shard back. What was the point of letting any of this happen? Of letting us..." She motioned back and forth between them, choking back a sob.

Piers sat beside her. He took her hand. "*Kardoula mou*." He brushed his lips over her knuckles. "The gods don't work that way. There's nothing straightforward about their machinations. They arrange, nudge, influence, sometimes shove. But it's all with a *potential* outcome in mind. After, it's up to us, their players and pawns, to make our choices and move our pieces around the board. If it all comes together the way the gods desire, then it's done, and they move on to something else. If it doesn't, they begin again with a new set of players who make their own moves, just as we did."

Tears shimmered in her eyes as she looked at him. "I never thought of there being a balance between fate and free will. I never even believed in destiny, but now..."

Piers gently kissed her. "I don't know if there's a balance, but it's not all or nothing. It's both."

She nodded. It was unsteady and forced. "So this is it? I should call my parents. Say goodbye. Just in case." Her voice broke, and Piers's heart crumbled to dust.

"No, my love. You get in your car and go home." He glanced at Sophie's phone again. "You said it takes about three hours? That's how long I'll wait. Then I'll summon Athena and give her the shard."

Sophie sniffled, straightening. "But I have to check us out of the hotel. No." She shook her head. "No, Piers. None of this works."

"I have at least thirty gold coins. Surely, the hotel can find a way to exchange them for little green papers and settle this debt. I'll leave the money in the bathroom." He grimaced, regretting his fit of temper. He could've left that gold with Sophie instead.

Piers unbuckled his belt and slipped the leather pouch from it. Rising, he strode to the bathroom and set the coin purse on the counter, hoping there would be steaming-hot showers wherever he ended up next. After Sophie, they were what he liked best about this place.

Returning to the main room, he sat beside her again. "The gold just needs to be turned into a useable currency. You can leave without worry."

"Leave without worry?" She frowned at him. "What if you *don't* get taken? What will you do then?"

He reached for her phone. "Call you. Show me how."

Her lips thinned. Then she took the phone from him. "Assuming *I* don't get taken, either, you'll have to dial my home number if I leave my cell phone with you." She opened *Contacts*, scrolled to *House*, and showed him how to launch the communication. "If I don't answer, leave a message. I'll come back and get you. I can be back tonight."

"Tonight is Christmas Eve. It seems special to you. You'll spend it with your family." He hoped.

"I don't care if it's the freaking apocalypse. I'll come back for you."

Piers's heart swooped in his chest. "We'll meet again, *Sophronia mou*. In this life, or in the next."

She shivered at his words. "Maybe the gods will be merciful," she whispered, her voice thick with tears.

Piers drank in the sight of her, memorizing every detail of her face. His soul recognized her as his, but what that really meant was that he was *hers*.

"Maybe." It was his deepest wish. More so than even to return home. Sophie was his home now.

They reached for each other, and there were no more words. There were long kisses and tender touches. There was breath-stealing passion that might have to last them a lifetime, until they met again in the Underworld.

Piers watched the snow fall outside and waited for the call that would change everything. It wasn't the one he'd made earlier. That had taken some trial and error, but he'd finally reached Novalight Enterprises and then the all-powerful man himself—after a long time spent persuading person after person that *Mr.* Novalight *really* wanted to talk to him.

Sophie had left nearly three hours ago, and Piers still felt as though a Cyclops sat on his chest, the crushing weight keeping his lungs from expanding. His heart seemed to beat out her name, and he couldn't stop thinking about how she'd stopped him from using one of her little sheaths when they made love. She hadn't wanted it. Maybe they both hoped he'd left a part of himself with her. Although the idea of his child growing up without him made Piers's stomach plummet. But Sophie... She could handle anything. The week she'd just endured would've broken a lesser woman. She would persevere. She would *thrive*.

The hotel phone rang, and Piers nearly jumped out of his skin. His pulse pounding, he picked up the handle and put it to his ear. "Yes?"

"There's a man here to see you. Mr. Smith."

Mr. *Novalight* Smith. Piers picked up his sword. "Thank you. You can send him to the room."

If the next few minutes didn't go as Piers hoped, the last thing he would do on this world would be to run Novalight through. The billionaire scientist wouldn't bother Sophie again—because Piers had no doubt the man would try to study and use her abilities, with or without the Shard of Olympus to make them work.

Earlier, he'd made sure people in the lobby had seen Sophie leave, her luggage in hand. He'd spoken to the concierge about the Christmas tree in Rockefeller Center, just so the man would remember seeing her go. He'd even gone back to the desk and told them he was staying one more night on his own and would take care of checkout in the morning. Piers had watched enough of this *news channel* during the afternoon to know that killing people, even dangerous ones, carried a different weight here than it did in Thalyria.

Systems in this place kept people accountable in ways he'd never seen in his life, and he wanted to make damn sure no one could blame Sophie for the dead man in their room.

Between the slow elevators and long corridors, it would take Novalight several minutes to get here. Hopefully, just on time.

Piers started chanting.

Call a god, lose a soul. He couldn't believe he was doing this again. He knew it brought misery. But he also believed it would keep Sophie safe. And put the shard back where it belonged.

Power gathered in the air around him. The chant required several repetitions. He spoke faster, louder. The windows frosted over, filtering out the day's last light and the gently falling snow.

Piers started the final repetition. Would he even remember his time on Earth after Athena took him? Would he remember Sophie?

Yes, by gods. She'd burned herself into his soul.

He ended the chant and spoke the name of the goddess who put him here to begin with. "Athena!"

Golden light swirled in the room. It heated the air and melted the frost on the windows. Athena slipped out of the sunlit glow and regarded him with interest. She was a good foot taller than Piers even with her head cocked to one side. She wore a flowing white gown as opposed to the armor he'd last seen her in. Perhaps in New York, she had no need for her spear and shield. Piers couldn't help staring in awe. He didn't blame anyone but himself for his exile from Thalyria, and he almost wanted to thank Athena for bringing him to Sophie.

A small smile curved her lips, and her golden-brown eyes softened, as if she'd read his thoughts. The radiance around her disappeared, leaving only the electric lights. Athena outshined them all. "Piers of Sinta. You summon an Olympian again. Are you foolhardy or brave?"

Piers bowed his head. "Neither, I think. But I saw no other way."

"Call a god, lose a soul. Is that not what you learned?"

"It is." He lifted his hand, palm up, and presented the Shard of Olympus. Sophie had been able to wear it, though it burned his hand with cold. "But this was in danger of falling into the wrong hands, and it was putting an innocent woman and her family at risk."

Athena hummed in the back of her throat. "Indeed, it was." She reached out, and the shard floated from his hand to hers. Piers watched in wonder as she tucked it inside her chest, passing it through her skin and bones. The glacial-blue glow illuminated her from the inside out before disappearing, swallowed whole.

Piers let out an unsteady breath. A knock sounded at the door.

"In terms of losing a soul, I have an option to present." He moved toward the door. "I know it's not my choice, but please consider who caused the trouble here."

Piers opened the door. Novalight stood there, looking ready to take what he believed was his. He'd come alone, as requested. Maybe his ruffians were down the hall. Piers didn't care. He pulled him inside and shut the door.

"You're not Sophronia Iraklidis." Novalight glared beyond Piers's shoulder.

Piers turned, and his jaw slid ajar. Athena now wore an outfit much like Sophie's—slim-fitting jeans and a loose sweater that hung off one shoulder, something strappy underneath, and bright Christmas socks on her feet. She'd shrunk, though she remained tall. Her tight, upswept curls had given way to long, loose waves that tumbled to her waist. She could sit in a New York restaurant and fit in just like anyone else. Piers snapped his mouth shut. Maybe she did sometimes.

"I hear you've been terrorizing a young woman," Athena said. Even her voice had changed, losing power and resonance. She sounded human and reminded him so much of Sophie, it hurt. The two females could be friends. Family. In a way, they were.

"I've been trying to get back what's mine from a *thief*. Are you a thief, too?" Novalight demanded.

"What's *yours*?" Athena laughed, the sound like shattered glass falling from a skyscraper. Her human veneer cracked, hinting at the deity beneath. "You speak awfully boldly for a man who doesn't know what he's talking about."

Color mottled Novalight's cheeks. "And who are you?"

Athena's smile turned blade sharp. Maybe she couldn't fit into the city that easily after all. "I'm the one who knows who that...crystal...really belongs to. It belongs to my father. I'm taking it to him."

Novalight barked a laugh.

Athena looked far from amused, and Piers drew his

sword, flanking her in the now-crowded room. Novalight looked at Piers's weapon with disdain, maybe thinking it was a fake. Then his breathing changed.

Piers smiled. *That's right. Not a toy.* Novalight had scared Sophie. He deserved to know fear in return.

Piers didn't want him dead, though. Novalight was his alternate solution in this game of bargaining souls.

"If someone must be taken, then why not take him? Maybe you could give him to Ares," Piers cautiously suggested. "See how well he fares?" That would've been Kaia's fate if Piers hadn't offered to take her place. Ares had accepted, but then Athena swooped in and snatched Piers for this. Ares was down one soul he should've commanded, and Novalight could be it.

Athena pursed her lips. "Unfortunately, that's not possible. The Moirai have decreed his bloodline too important to future events. He must go on to produce children here on Earth."

Piers's heart sank. Not even Zeus could overrule the will of the Fates. So, this was it. It would be him.

Or gods forbid, Sophie.

"Here on Earth? What are you two lunatics talking about?" Novalight's wary gaze darted over them both, then to Piers's sword again.

"We're talking about life and death, the fate of men in the cosmos, and the role of destiny," Athena said blithely. "And really, this world considers him a genius?" She rolled her eyes.

Piers barely registered her scorn. His gut had turned to stone the moment his bargaining chip got swept off the table. His only concern now was Sophie and *her* life—making sure she lived it in peace.

Novalight chose that moment to lunge at him. Piers brought the hilt of his sword up whip-fast and cracked him in the face. This journey had begun with a broken nose. It might as well end with one.

Novalight reeled back with a gasp. Piers's mouth twisted in disgust. He didn't even hit him that hard. And if Athena couldn't take the bastard to another world or let Piers kill him, how would Sophie ever be safe?

Desperation filled him. Piers prided himself on solving problems, but he didn't know how to solve this. All the book learning and battle experience of his life couldn't free Sophie from a man protected by the Fates.

Nevertheless, he took a menacing step toward Novalight. "How do *you* like being faced with someone bigger and scarier?" he ground out. "Think about how Sophie felt when you sent your men after her again and again."

Novalight hyperventilated, sucking in blood and half choking on it as he backed toward the door.

Glaring at Piers, Athena cocked out a jean-clad hip and flicked her hand toward the scientist. "Now I have to fix that."

Fury and confusion clashed like cymbals in Piers's head. Who *was* this goddess? Not the Athena he…really didn't know. He stopped in his tracks.

A noise clicked behind Novalight, the door flew open, and Sophie burst into the room.

"No!" Piers shouted.

"Yes!" Athena clapped.

"You!" Novalight grabbed her and dragged her against his chest.

Piers reacted on pure instinct. He freed Sophie from Novalight's hold with a sharp downward strike, spun her out of the way, and threw the man against the wall so hard the son of a Cyclops shattered the plaster and dropped.

"Ugh. Now I have to fix *that*." Athena scowled at him again. "And the bathroom. You're in Attica now, so you need to get something through your thick, Thalyrian, he-man-warrior head. Destruction and maiming: *bad*. Piers and Sophie live happily ever after: *good*."

"But…" Piers's heart pounded. He kept an eye on the unconscious Novalight as he reached for Sophie. "Call a god, lose a soul. One of us…" He gripped Sophie tighter, whispering to her, "You shouldn't have come back."

"I had to." She wrapped her arms around him. "I couldn't just leave you."

"You should've." Athena wasn't the only danger here. There was Novalight—not that Sophie had known that.

Athena fluffed her hair. "The Fates say I can't have Novalight—although I think he'd make a fun tool for Hephaestus or good target practice for Artemis. Lucky for you both: different place, different rules." Her mouth quirked up. "I'm not *technically* bound to take a soul from Attica. Thalyria is the only place where that rule is set in stone. People there wanted Olympians to intervene entirely too much. It was getting out of hand and had to be controlled."

Shock and cautious hope tightened every muscle in Piers's body. Summoning had definitely been controlled.

Those scrolls had been *buried*. And the information half lost and easily misunderstood.

"Are you saying…we're free?" He hesitated to understand—in case he *didn't*. He feared a trick that would leave him devastated.

Athena's head swiveled toward Novalight, sliding in a way that reminded him she wasn't at all human. "Oh, I can do better than that."

A stick appeared in her hand. She waved it. "Bibbidi-bobbidi-boo." Athena winked at Sophie. "I've always wanted to say that. Or at least, for the last seventy years or so."

Novalight rose to his feet like a ragdoll. Athena spun him around several times with glittering, swirling magic, bringing him back to consciousness and fixing his nose. She hit him over the head with her stick, and he disappeared.

Piers blinked hard, making sure the man was really gone. Sophie's relieved laughter unraveled the knots in his chest.

"That was all for show." Athena grinned, especially at Sophie. "I couldn't resist."

"What happened to him?" Sophie asked, smiling back.

"He's back in his house on Christmas eve, contemplating calling the woman he'll eventually make those fated babies with, and not remembering a single thing about either of you or the Shard of Olympus. The whole thing never happened. His hired guns have no idea why they were out and about and getting pummeled in New York. His archeological site in the Mediterranean turned out to be a complete dud, and he'll sell the entire island tomorrow to a professional soccer player from England who's about to retire."

Piers understood only parts of that, but Sophie nodded, appearing to like the plan.

"That's brilliant. Thank you." Sophie blushed. Athena might seem less intimidating masquerading as a thirty-something New Yorker, but she was still an Olympian and radiated power.

Athena looked at Sophie almost with affection. "You won't have your magic without the Shard of Olympus. The shard was dormant, like all magic here, until it encountered *Heracleidae*. Aaron first, although his blood was very diluted. The shard spoke to him just enough to spark some research into his ancient lineage—and yours. The magic is far stronger in your blood."

"I don't want magic." Sophie shuddered. "It terrifies me."

"As it should." Athena sighed. "The people of Earth have invented terrible enough weapons as it is. Magic has no place here."

Sophie murmured her agreement as she tucked herself into Piers's side.

"What happens next?" Piers asked, still fearing a trick in the end. He wouldn't put it past Athena to let the other shoe drop now and kick him in the head.

The goddess tsked at him, chuckling under her breath. Then she waved her magic stick again. Several things appeared on the bed. "Well, you're still exiled—sorry. Can't change that."

Piers wasn't sorry. Not with Sophie by his side. Not with the life he could imagine for them.

"So, here's a birth certificate, passport, driver's license, and university diploma—three in fact, including one from Oxford." She handed him several papers, a hard little rectangle with his image on it, and a small blue book. "You own a highly successful auction house in Connecticut that restores, appraises, and sells ancient artifacts from around the world, particularly the Mediterranean basin. Here's the deed to the warehouse and showroom." She handed him something else. "You're well-known in your field and regularly asked to consult on anything pertaining to antiquities. However, you read nothing but academic works and really need to branch out. I suggest Nora Roberts." Athena handed him a paperback.

Sophie gasped. "I have the rest of that series!"

"I know." Athena smirked. "That's the brand-new release."

Overwhelmed by gratitude and relief, Piers could only smile and shake his head while the women talked about something called *binge-watching*. He only partially listened, his mind already focused ahead and happiness welling in his chest. Sophie and he had served their goddess well, and she'd rewarded them. He was still half lost, but he knew he'd catch on fast, especially with Sophie guiding him through every day of this new life.

EPILOGUE

Four years later, Pinebury, Connecticut

Piers rubbed his hands together, smiling at a job well done. The Christmas tree was up, the girls were sticky with candy-cane sugar—including Sophie—and he'd finally gotten that stubborn cord of colored lights to work. Met and Moma, their two Golden Retrievers, had only broken one ornament this year so far with their excitedly thumping tails, which seemed a vast improvement over last year's carnage when they'd still been puppies.

Met licked sugar off Athena's face while she giggled, and Moma was doing the same to little Zoe's fingers. In the grand tradition of the Iraklidis of Connecticut, they'd given their children Greek names. Athena, after the goddess, and Zoe, meaning life. It had seemed only fitting to both him and Sophie, since Athena had given them this life they were living.

"Who wants to put the star on?" Piers held up the sparkly golden topping for their Christmas tree.

Both girls jumped up. "Me! Me! Daddy, me!"

Piers's heart grew so big in his chest that it pushed against his ribs. He sometimes still wished his Thalyrian family could see who he'd become and what he'd accomplished, but what he had here in Pinebury—including the extended family that would be arriving soon to "bake the boosh" for Sophie's last week of school before Christmas—made any loss and heartbreak he'd suffered worth it. Regrets were real, especially concerning Griffin and Cat, but he wouldn't change anything. His choices brought him here. To Sophie. To Athena and Zoe.

Clearing the rising thickness from his throat, he smiled at his girls. "Well, I guess it's both of you, then." He hoisted a daughter onto each shoulder.

"Piers..." Sophie gave him a *Be careful* look, but he just grinned at her. There was no way in the Underworld he would drop his children.

"Hold on." Sophie popped up from patting the dogs and getting her own sticky fingers licked. "I'll get the camera."

She came back with her phone and started snapping

pictures. Piers got Athena and Zoe to both hold the star and leaned in, helping Zoe with her shorter arms and more questionable balance.

"It's on!" Athena squealed in delight.

"On! On!" Zoe chanted. Her wet little fingers smacked Piers in the eye, and he blinked, grinning.

"Get ready for landing," he announced, pretending to be an airplane until he reached the living room couch and gently tumbled them onto it.

The dogs immediately joined the girls. Where the girls went, the dogs followed. Athena buried her face in Moma's neck and started kissing.

Sophie watched them play, taking more pictures, before turning her smiling gaze on the Christmas tree again. Piers joined her, giving the tall, full tree a satisfied onceover.

"I think it's our prettiest tree yet," Sophie said, resting her head on his shoulder.

Piers looped his arm around her. "Maybe we should get two next year. Really spruce up the living room." He waited for it.

Sophie let out a groan. She laughed, too, though. "That is *such* a dad joke."

"I'll take that as a compliment." He chuckled.

She rolled her eyes, teasing, "You're lucky I love you."

"I know I'm lucky." He kissed her. "I love you, too." So much his heart burned with it.

She sighed happily, snuggling against him. "The star looks nice."

Piers nodded. It did. It was also crooked and had

candy-cane fingerprints on it. "This will be our fifth Christmas together." It was amazing how time flew, even without realms to conquer and bloodbath battles to get into. He was glad they'd maintained Sophie's holiday traditions. She now knew the gods of Olympus were more than myth, but they didn't reign here and hadn't for millennia. She'd maintained her faith while recognizing that other powerful forces existed in the universe. But when they told stories from Greek mythology to their children, they treated them as a bit more than fiction. Piers scattered in tales about his family as though they came from ancient times, too, and were long-lost ancestors, just like Heracles. It was the only way for his girls to know their other aunts and uncles and grandparents.

The doorbell rang. The dogs started barking.

"Auntie Xanthe's here with Ya-Ya!" Athena cried.

"Ya-Ya!" Zoe echoed.

The girls ran to the door—well, one toddled—along with Met and Moma. Piers could've sworn Met held back to help Zoe along and let the little girl, whose fist curled into her coat, use her sturdy frame for balance.

"You're helping us bake the *Bûches de Noël* this year!" Sophie called after their daughters. "You, too." She squeezed Piers's waist, gazing up at the bright Christmas star one last time before the door flew open and all hell broke loose for the entire weekend.

Piers smiled. He couldn't wait. The cozy red house would smell like mulled cider, cake, and chocolate, the family would laugh and tease and gossip, especially when

Pappou and Sophie's brothers—some with wives and children now—showed up "unexpectedly" for dinner, and Piers would know he'd ended up exactly where he was meant to be when the Fates decided on *his* future.

A NOTE TO READERS

Dear Reader,

I hope you enjoyed *Of Fate and Fire*. If you'd like to find out more about Cat and Griffin and their epic adventures in Thalyria, I hope you'll check out The Kingmaker Chronicles. You can also find out more about Piers's family and friends in a brand-new novel, *A Curse of Queens*, coming next in that exciting fantasy world.

Curious about what happens with Novalight's family? You can find out just how terrifying one of his descendants becomes as rebel captain Tess Bailey and her crew of Robin Hood-like thieves fight him and his oppressive regime for all they're worth in the steamy and action-packed Nightchaser series.

Thank you for reading!

To find out more about my books and sign up for my newsletter, please visit www.amandabouchet.com.

EXCERPT FROM A CURSE FOR SPRING

A malevolent spell strangles the kingdom of Leathen in catastrophic drought. Prince Daric must break the curse before his people starve. A once-mighty goddess trapped in a human body might be the key—but saving his kingdom could mean losing all that he loves.

PROLOGUE

Prince Daric touched his fingers to the giant column of mist and then jerked them back. He stared at his fingertips, but nothing had changed. His skin hadn't reddened; the nails weren't blackened. Nothing, in fact, had happened.

With a nervous swallow scraping down his throat, he turned his head to check that no one had followed him from the royal encampment. The dying forest stared back with gnarled eyes, everything brittle, creaking, and ready to catch fire. Nothing disturbed the too-dry branches, but it was only a matter of time before someone noticed he'd snuck off and came looking for him.

They were still days from home after a long journey to neighboring Raana followed by a pilgrimage to their own sacred Wood of Layton. Negotiations with Raana's Royal House of Nighthall had not gone well, putting everyone in a foul mood, especially Daric's father. King Wilder worried for his people, and Queen Illanna Nighthall had shown more greed than humanity, as usual.

Every year had been the same since Daric's birth—ten years of drought. Fields grew drier, the people of Leathen thinner, and the royal coffers lighter as Daric's parents were forced to pay the surrounding kingdoms for water, grains, and provisions.

After another look around him to make sure all was quiet, Daric turned back to Braylian's Cauldron. A thick column of mist rose from the sacred circle, but he knew that at any second, the elements could shift, turning into violent flames, bolts of lightning fierce enough to blind a man, gales that whipped and wailed, or shards of ice that exploded upward before raining down like daggers.

Children were warned away from the Cauldron from the moment they could understand fear. At least once a year, Daric joined the rest of the royal family at the volatile stone-lined circle to pay homage to Braylian, the goddess of the elements and the divine creator of the four seasons.

Usually, he was not alone to come before Braylian and beg for the return of water to Leathen's lakes and rivers. And to his knowledge, no one had ever stood this close to the Cauldron. He was not too young to understand the consequences of this ongoing lack of true springtime. He saw the tension in his parents and the gauntness of his people. The fact that he and the drought were the same age made him even more determined to find a solution. Somehow, he felt responsible.

Gathering his courage, Daric stretched his hand into

the mist again, this time losing sight of everything up to his wrist. It was cool, damp, and terrifying. He curled his hand into a fist and drew back. As he did, he could have sworn he felt a soft brush of fingers across his knuckles.

Daric shivered in a way he knew a brave young prince shouldn't, and had he been a hallerhound, he'd have felt the hair on the back of his neck rise and quiver.

He squared his shoulders. Raana coveted Leathen's orin mines. No longer satisfied with simply purchasing the strong, versatile metal, Illanna Nighthall had just successfully bartered for a nearly untapped mine that hugged the border. She had one shaft now. Next year, Daric feared she would have another.

Why spring rains would still water and nurture the surrounding kingdoms but not Leathen was a mystery. All Daric knew was that Leathen had faithfully guarded Braylian's Cauldron for generations. It was time that Braylian returned the favor for Leathen.

"Braylian!" he called out, frightened, even though the stone circle seemed calm today. This was where spirits gathered, the seasons changed, and storms were born from nothing. "We need your help!"

No response came, and the mist remained quiet. He leaned forward, dipping his head into the column. To do so was bold and spine-chilling, but if the goddess saw him, maybe she would answer.

A thick gray cloud dampened Daric's skin with more wetness than he'd felt on his face outside of his own washroom since the last snows of winter, but he saw only fog in front of him.

Disappointed but also a little relieved, he straightened out of the column. Leathen's summer heat sucked the moisture from the land, its autumn storms sometimes ruined the crops the kingdom's struggling farmers managed to cultivate, and its harsh winter freezes left too many people huddled around kitchen fires, cold and hungry. The long, ground-watering rains of springtime had abandoned Leathen the moment Daric came into it.

He didn't know how, or why, but he needed to fix it before the drought forced his parents to sell their kingdom piece by piece to the power-hungry Queen of Raana.

An orin mine for water. More orinore for bread. When Leathen had no riches left, what would become of it?

Other kingdoms would turn covetous looks their way soon, just as Raana did. Land was land, even if it was dead.

Daric appealed to the goddess again, leaning once more into the mist. He knew his actions were dangerous. Reckless, even. But what good was a prince to a kingdom that might cease to exist?

He called to Braylian until he was hoarse. Finally forced to admit defeat, he withdrew his head and torso from the cloud and started back toward the royal camp, his heart heavy with failure.

A lilting female voice stopped him in his tracks. "Who calls?"

The sound was more water than words. Daric turned back in awe, seeing a hand emerge from the column. Small fingers mirrored the tentative movements he'd first made into the mist. As if she'd learned from him, she mimicked his gestures, eventually leaning forward. As she did, her upper body took form, solidifying. Every action matched his, except she was a girl. She was even his age, and the most ethereal, radiant being he'd ever seen.

She stretched out her hand more boldly. Beads of water dripped from her fingertips. *Rain*. It watered the dying ground between them, turning it vibrant and green.

Daric moved toward the Cauldron, his eyes wide and his pulse beating with wild hope. "I am Daric, of the House of Ash. Are you Braylian?"

"I am her daughter," she answered. Her speech was slow, as if she were discovering language as they talked.

At the dawn of time, Braylian created the four seasons to help her govern the year. This daughter had new vines for clothing, silver waterfalls for hair, and eyes the color of the lakes he'd seen in Raana.

Spring! She had to be Spring! And she had not yet gone to her rest. This was her last day of the season. At dawn, Summer rose from her bed.

"Why have you abandoned my kingdom?" Daric asked. "Will you not water our fields again?"

"I have abandoned no kingdom," she replied. "I water all the lands that I see."

Daric frowned. "Then...do you not see Leathen?"

She looked as confused as he. She seemed to have no answer and withdrew into the Cauldron again.

"Please!" Daric dashed after her. He stepped partway into the misty column, forgetting about the stone circle he wasn't supposed to cross. "Can you see me? Can you see my kingdom?"

A vague form twirled in the cloud, rushing like a river,

swirling like a tempest. He moved toward the shadow, and an icy sheet of water splashed across his face. He jerked back with a gasp.

"Do not step through, or you can never go back," she warned. "Braylian will claim you, and you will race across the land and sky as weather."

Daric retreated, his heart pounding in fright. The girl followed him halfway out. They began a gentle back and forth, almost a dance. She met his gaze, and her delighted smile put to shame the most beautiful of starlit nights.

"We're in a terrible drought," he said as they continued to sway together, sometimes Daric partway into the Cauldron, sometimes her partway out. "Can you help us?"

She threw a high-arching spray of water into the forest with a tinkling laugh.

"That's wonderful." Daric grinned. "But we need much more than that."

She shook her head. "I see only you and the magic of the Cauldron. Everything else is dark."

Hard hands suddenly ripped Daric away from her. He struggled but was no match for the large man dragging him back. He recognized Soren's gruff voice as his father's personal guard banded a heavy arm around his chest and told him to settle.

As though Soren's words broke a spell, people appeared around him. His mother stood only a step away, pale with terror. Beside her, his father swung a calculating gaze back and forth between Daric and the girl, the gears of his mind visibly turning.

"No!" cried Daric a split second before King Wilder

surged forward and clamped his hand around the girl's wrist. With a decisive yank, he pulled her from the Cauldron.

She turned entirely to flesh as she crossed the stone circle. The vines covering her milky-white skin withered and died. Her silver hair stopped cascading water. Her eyes were the only part of her that still brimmed with moisture, and she stood there, shaking.

Daric shoved away from Soren and ran to her, throwing his cloak around her shoulders. He tugged it closed to cover her, and she clutched at the garment, her legs trembling like a newborn foal's. She seemed barely able to hold up her weight, even though she was as slight as a sapling.

"Can you make it rain, child?" the king asked urgently, bending down close to her. "I will give you all that I have for rain."

She blinked at Daric's father, silent, and yet everything about her screamed out in horror. The tears in her eyes hit the ground, but they made no difference to the crisp brown moss still struggling to survive in Leathen's sacred forest.

Daric began to shake along with her. He'd failed, and he'd ruined spring forever.

She'd seen only him, and Daric only her. Some magic had blinded them, a curse for spring, and him, and everyone.

"Rain," he pleaded softly. Maybe she could still control the elements. Maybe she was still Braylian's daughter.

Sorrow filled the bluest eyes he'd ever seen. "Once, I might have been what you needed. Now, I am nothing."

A CURSE FOR SPRING: CHAPTER 1

CHAPTER 1

"Rain? Are you awake?"

Rain cracked open her eyes at the sound of Daric's deep voice. Her lungs squeezed with joy and relief that he was home safely from his latest trip up and down the slippery Axton Peaks, although she simply mumbled something that sounded like *No* while her heart settled into a normal beat.

Daric slipped into her room anyway and stretched out beside her on the high bed. He was lying down but hardly still. Her prince was a constant explosion of motion, going everywhere as if his heels were on fire.

And he called *her* the storm.

"Happy birthday!" Daric turned onto his side, beaming at her.

"I'm sleeping." Rain refused to open her eyes enough to do more than watch him through her lashes. The day her adoptive parents had chosen as her birthday was a terrible day. It was the first morning of spring, and another long season of *nothing*. "But welcome home," she said with a budding smile.

"You're not sleeping. You're talking to me."

She huffed, unable to fault his logic. "We're not children anymore. You *do* know that it's highly inappropriate for you to charge into my bedroom like this? Especially at the crack of dawn."

"The crack of dawn?" Daric scoffed. "That was at least three minutes ago."

"You're impossible." Sighing, Rain resigned herself to facing the day—this day when everyone still hoped she'd do something amazing and wonderful, even though they'd stopped expecting it a long time ago.

At least Daric was back, which made it all more bearable.

She stretched the sleep from her limbs and opened her eyes, allowing herself to really look at him. Her chest knotted with the usual mix of elation, misery, and longing. His face was weathered from his latest journey, maybe even a little sun-scorched, and his blue eyes stood out with brilliance against his tanned skin. His dark hair had grown, now tumbling over his forehead in a way that made her want to smooth it between her fingers and brush it back. And his smile...

Rain's pulse sped up again. His smile was the same as always: warm and devastating.

"Did everything go well?" she asked.

Daric nodded. "The last two towns in the dry-belt now have their full supply of ice blocks. I inspected the containers, and they're all in good shape. It won't water their fields, but it'll give the townsfolk what they need to survive the upcoming season."

Several years ago, Daric had conceived of a plan to

provide extra water for the towns around Leathen with the fewest natural depressions to collect rainwater and snowmelt from the winter. Under his direction, villagers had built huge watertight basins to hold blocks of ice that Daric and a team of soldiers regularly cut from the mountain lakes in winter. Each journey meant a difficult climb into the Axton Peaks, a long week of perilous work, and a treacherous descent with heavy sleds stacked with ice. While the weather was still cold enough to transport the frozen water, Daric brought it to the towns that needed it the most. There, it was stored and slowly melted as the weather warmed. With rationing, the ice provided enough water for areas hovering on the brink of disaster to survive the inevitably rainless spring while everyone waited for summer storms to help refill their water towers.

Daric had yet to lose a man on these dangerous but necessary outings, and Rain knew he'd jumped into holes in the ice more than once to pull someone out. People didn't die on Daric's watch, despite the winter elements sometimes doing their best to blow his team from the mountaintops. Rain felt as though she held her breath each time he left and only let it out again when he returned.

"Did you just arrive?" she asked.

"Last night," he answered. "But you'd already gone to bed."

That explained why he was clean-shaven and looked freshly washed. Polite and civilized were expected of Daric, but Rain enjoyed seeing him come home all bristly and wind-whipped and looking deliciously barbarous in his winter furs. Weapons strapped on. Somehow stronger and wider after each grueling, work-filled expedition. Eyes sparking blue fire from across the room.

She shivered just thinking about it, although with him beside her, she was anything but cold.

Rain sat up and wiggled back against the headboard. Daric did the same and then handed her a small box.

He grinned at her. "I would have offered you a silver necklace to match your hair, a sapphire ring to match your eyes, or a ruby brooch to match your lips, but Leathen has no riches left, so you'll have to make do with this." He tapped the lid of the box, his smile widening.

Rain smiled back, laughing a little. "You make me sound like a crown—silver and rubies and sapphires."

"Sadly, we don't have a single crown anymore, either. Besides, they were all gold, and you certainly don't have boring yellow hair."

The mood in the dawn-lit room abruptly soured as they both thought about who *did* have blonde hair—Astraea Nighthall.

"You don't have to marry her," Rain murmured, turning the unopened gift over in her hands. She watched the box, unable to look at Daric again yet. The near constant ache in her chest ratcheted up with a vengeance. She'd thought her heart hurt before? Lately, it was in constant pain.

"And do what?" Daric asked bitterly, some of the princely veneer slipping from his voice. "Run away?"

Steeling herself, Rain turned back to him. "Talk to your father. He can't possibly wish her on you." Astraea Nighthall was all that was spiteful, vicious, and petty.

Daric shook his head. "The contract has been negotiated. We marry. Our first child inherits both kingdoms. Raanaleath." He snorted. "It sounds like a disease."

Angry, unhappy Daric felt like a stranger by her side. These past few months, though, this surly prince had become more familiar to her. "At least Leathen won't be obliterated from the name entirely." Not like the name of Ash, which they were being forced to abandon.

He tried to smile and failed utterly. "Good point, Raindrop." Rain watched as he drew a deep breath and forced back his visible dread over the future that was slowly destroying them both. "Now open your present."

Rain swallowed the lump in her throat. If Daric could focus on today then she could, too. It was better than thinking about the vile Astraea in his bed.

She rubbed the velvet-covered box between her fingers. It was a daring red. She wasn't surprised Daric had chosen something he knew she'd like, even if the color was better suited to an experienced, married woman.

"I'm not certain today's a day to celebrate," Rain said.

He drew back, his countenance darkening again. "You're not to blame for any of this."

"Neither are you," she shot back. "And yet you'll be punished for a lifetime."

"If I hadn't dragged you from the Cauldron, you'd still be Spring. You'd still control the elements, make rain and wind and grow new buds into trees." He shook his head, his features contorting into something she saw more and more often these days—disgust.

Rain knew it wasn't directed at her, but it still hurt to

see. She feared Daric would never stop blaming himself for what had happened. Not only to her, but the drought, the failing farms, the hungry people, the empty coffers, their dependence on Raana... Everything.

"*You* did not drag me from the Cauldron," she corrected.

"But my father..."

Rain put a finger over Daric's lips to hush him, warmth tingling down her arm at the contact. "King Wilder did what he thought was best, and I don't blame him, either. Your parents have been kind to me and have treated me as their own for the last fifteen years, despite my being a useless mouth to feed in their home."

"Useless mouth to feed?" Daric echoed indignantly.

His breath swirled around her finger, and the feel of his warm lips was one of the most intimate things Rain had ever experienced. Though they did almost everything together, they rarely touched except when dancing. But no one really danced anymore. There wasn't much to celebrate.

Rain dropped her hand. She remembered little of her life before she became flesh. She'd been ancient; she knew that. But she'd taken the form of a child to match the charming, earnest boy who'd called out to her that day. Awareness of her previous existence and abilities had been mostly stripped from her, and Braylian had refused to take her back into the Cauldron.

"What good am I?" she asked, knowing her tone matched Daric's recent bitterness. "Braylian brought forth a new Spring, and she doesn't see Leathen any more than I did. People are desperate and starving. I'm of no value to the kingdom. You're being forced to marry Astraea." Rain heard the near growl in her voice and didn't even try to disguise it. Raana's princess had been malicious as a child and age had only worsened her. On a royal visit many years ago, Astraea had snuck into Rain's bedroom one night and cut off her hair while she slept. She'd then used Rain's hair to make a noose to hang Daric's cat. Astraea still gloated about it. *That* was who Daric was being forced to marry. *That* was who he'd have to endure so that Raana would create a canal to divert water directly into Leathen.

Raana's mightiest reservoir sat mockingly on the border, filled to the brim with precious water. All they needed was a year of digging to direct some of that water into the dry riverbed that wound like a desiccated serpent through Leathen's once-fertile farmland.

King Wilder had been trying to negotiate a canal with Raana for years, but Illanna Nighthall wouldn't agree to it, even when orin mines had still been a valuable bargaining chip. She finally had, but her price was Daric. With a marriage, the House of Nighthall gained the heart of the continent, and Daric could finally save his people, if not his kingdom. His entire life revolved around bringing them out of this seemingly endless drought. He would do it, even if it meant tying himself to that witch Astraea.

"You're of value to me," Daric said softly.

Rain bit her lip to keep from saying—or perhaps doing—something rash. In moments like this, she wished that Daric would lean in and kiss her. And if he didn't, that maybe she would find the courage to kiss him.

She let the thought seduce her and then pushed it away, as always. "And you're of value to everyone."

A shadow flitted through his eyes, the cloud of responsibility, and she wished she'd said nothing.

"Let's talk of happier things," Daric said briskly. "Open your present."

Rain brushed her fingers over the velvet again, wondering what could be inside. When Daric said Leathen had nothing left, he meant it. Even the castle had been mostly stripped of tapestries, rugs, and furnishings and was in terrible condition, making cold mornings like this difficult to face. In return for the food Leathen so desperately needed, their neighbors, and especially Raana, now had everything the House of Ash could possibly sell or barter.

King Wilder had finally been forced to offer up the last thing he had of value: Daric.

If Rain had truly been a member of the Ash family, she supposed she would have gone first, likely to the House of Lockwood in the south to guarantee their continued friendship and assistance. They were the only ones with a marriageable male royal: a king much older than she who'd been widowed for years and whose heirs were daughters.

Any of the Lockwood princesses would have been better for Daric than Astraea. Regrettably, they were all married and also offered nothing in the way of easily accessible water.

"Your patience far exceeds mine," Daric said, reaching for the box.

Rain twisted away from him with a smile. "Don't you dare. I'll open it. Right now, I'm savoring it."

"Savoring the box?" His winter-blue eyes glimmered with roguish charm. "That's older than I am, you know. I found it in a wardrobe. I'm reusing it."

"It's lovely."

"And we'll both be old and gray before you actually open it," he grumbled.

Rain took pity on the impatient prince and lifted the lid. Amid more red velvet lay a delicate starflower carved from white marble. Her breath caught. It was Braylian's mark.

"When I made it, I carved a small loop into the back so that you can slide a hairpin through it. See?" Daric pulled a hairpin from his pocket, picked up the starflower, and slipped the pin through the loop. Clearly, he'd planned ahead.

Rain watched his deft fingers as much as the sparkling gift, too overwhelmed to speak. Early morning sunlight poured through the window—long deprived of curtains now—and glinted off the crystalline stone, making it glitter like snow on a winter morning.

Daric gathered a portion of her hair and attached the gift above her ear. "Like a snowflake on ice," he said, smiling as he adjusted a few sleep-tumbled locks and smoothed them down.

Rain shivered, not used to anyone else's hands in her hair, and least of all Daric's. She pressed her lips together, trapping her tears in her throat.

"Don't you like it?" Daric asked, a worried crease forming between his brows.

Like it? She loved it. She loved him. It was torture.

"It's the most beautiful gift I've ever had," Rain finally answered in a voice that thickened with every word. "Thank you."

Daric seemed pleased with her response, but then his expression turned troubled once more. "Wear it now, while you can, because you'll have to hide it after we all move to Nighthall."

"Why?" Rain asked, the thought of their family being uprooted two moons from now to live among vipers making her stomach cramp.

"Because Astraea will take it. She's always been madly jealous of you."

"That's ridiculous." Rain touched the starflower, wanting to look at it again but not wanting to undo Daric's careful handiwork. "She's a princess. Rich, powerful, and if one can ignore her inner ugliness, quite attractive."

Daric made a face as he hopped off the bed and moved toward the door. "I can't ignore it. I have names for Astraea but saying them out loud would tarnish your image of my princely manners forever."

Rain's lips twitched. "I'm certain my imagination can supply them without your help."

Daric's eyes sparked with genuine humor, despite the terrible union he faced for the benefit of his people. "I'm leaving so you can get dressed and come face the frigid breakfast room with me."

Rain got goose bumps just thinking about it. Even firewood was scarce these days, and they mainly kept it for the evenings, for a small moment of comfort and peace. This winter had been darker and colder than most, and while it was officially spring now, Rain doubted the new season would bring much improvement. Gradual warming, yes, but no rain, of course. Thankfully, snowmelt would at least help fill the natural water basins for the coming weeks.

Daric turned back to her from the doorway. "As for Astraea being jealous, you're of the House of Ash, and she knows she'll never have what you have."

"What's that?" Rain asked, her heart jerking uncomfortably.

"A family that loves you." Daric left and shut the door behind him.

Rain didn't try to stop the wetness flooding her eyes. She would cry rivers if only her tears would make the crops grow again in Leathen.

Continue reading A CURSE FOR SPRING wherever
e-books are sold or borrow it from your local library!
Visit www.amandabouchet.com to find out more.

ABOUT THE AUTHOR

USA Today bestselling author Amanda Bouchet grew up in New England where she spent much of her time tromping around in the woods and making up grand adventures in her head. It was inevitable that one day she would start writing them down. Amanda writes fantasy romance and space opera romance and was a Goodreads Choice Awards top ten finalist for Best Debut in 2016 with her first novel, *A Promise of Fire*.

For more about Amanda and her writing, please visit her website at www.amandabouchet.com.

ALSO BY AMANDA BOUCHET

The Kingmaker Chronicles

A Promise of Fire (Book 1)

Breath of Fire (Book 2)

Heart on Fire (Book 3)

A Curse of Queens (Book 4, coming October 2022)

Nightchaser

Nightchaser (Book 1)

Starbreaker (Book 2)

Dawnmaker (Book 3, coming soon)

A Curse for Spring

Printed in Great Britain
by Amazon